Sky Pony

Sky Pony

Elaine Breault Hammond

The Acorn Press
Charlottetown
2010

P.O. Box 22024
Charlottetown, Prince Edward Island
C1A 9J2
acornpresscanada.com

Printed and Bound in Canada
Cover illustration by Pam Swainson
Cover and interior design by Matt Reid

Library and Archives Canada Cataloguing in Publication
  Hammond, Elaine Breault, 1937-
  Sky pony / Elaine Breault Hammond.
  ISBN 978-1-894838-51-1

I. Title.
PS8565.A566S59 2010   jC813'.54   C2010-905347-8

Canada Council   Conseil des Arts
for the Arts   du Canada

The publisher acknowledges the support of the Government of Canada through the Canada Book Fund of the Department of Canadian Heritage and the Canada Council for the Arts Block Grant Program.

FSC
Mixed Sources
Cert no. SW-COC-000952
© 1996 FSC

Thanks to my PEI writers' group, the Ladeez Auxiliary, for reading the manuscript and for helping to get it ready for publication. Thanks to my Kingston writers' group for their perceptive comments and suggestions. Most of all, thanks to Allan and our grown children, Rob, Greg, Julia, and Kirby for their constant support and encouragement.

— Chapter 1 —
Betrayal

They sat by a window that looked out on a lawn. A row of tall plastic ferns separated their table from the others. Dad smiled. Katie could tell because his eyes crinkled and she could see the ends of his moustache moving upward. For the first time, she noticed strands of grey in his beard and creases on his forehead.

"Go crazy," he said when she looked at the menu. "If you want pizza, so be it."

Katie was surprised. At home it was lentil soup or black bean stew or do without.

"Is it okay if I have a double chocolate sundae?"

"Be my guest."

But when the gooey dessert arrived, her throat closed and she couldn't eat. They're just trying to win me over, she thought. With this fancy motel and junk food for breakfast. They want me to say everything is okay. And nothing will ever be okay again.

Marc and Maggie didn't seem to notice that their daughter wasn't eating. They were nervously nibbling toast and drinking tons of black coffee. Mom kept looking out the window, as if something might suddenly appear on the lawn and she didn't want to miss it. The morning sun shone on her thin face, partly hidden by a lock of her straight brown hair. She pulled her hair behind her ear, but when she leaned forward to sip her coffee, a bit escaped and fell across her cheek again. Just like me, thought Katie, brushing her long, straight, brown hair back from her face.

They were in Winnipeg, on their way from Thunder Bay, Katie's home for all her nearly twelve years, to their new home in Whitehorse, Yukon. The end of the world, Katie thought. She had been against the move ever since her parents had told her about it months ago, but she didn't want to complain too much since she loved them and wanted to make them happy.

Maggie and Marc were modern parents. They had discussed every aspect of the move with their only child. They said they understood that she didn't want to leave her many friends and the school where she'd been so happy. They knew that she didn't want to leave the white stucco house with the steep gables where she'd lived all her life. But, as Dad explained, really good jobs for geologists were hard to find, especially for someone with a disability like his. This one in the Yukon was his dream job, and he'd be a fool not to jump at it. Besides, he had worked in the Yukon years ago, when he was young, and he had such good memories, he was anxious to go back.

Mom had found a college teaching job in Whitehorse, and that meant regular hours so she would have more time at home. "You just wait and see," she said. "You'll like Whitehorse just as much as Thunder Bay once you get settled in school and make friends." Katie knew her parents were proud of her and had a lot of confidence in her. She had always felt good about her family—until now.

Then Dad told Katie that a real estate agent had found a house for them in the countryside just outside Whitehorse, next door to a stable where people boarded horses. "Your birthday is coming up and what have you always wanted, ever since you were tiny?"

It was true. All her life, whenever she wished on a wishbone, she had wished for a pony. Whenever she made the first cut in the birthday cake, she had shut her eyes and wished for a horse. Katie's feelings about the move began to change just a smidgen.

Maybe she would have a different attitude if there really was a horse in her future. That hint was the crack of light at the end of a long, dark tunnel between her perfect, happy life and the strange new one they were headed for.

Katie pictured herself in a big country house surrounded by spruce trees tipped with snow, riding a dashing black stallion across the white frozen fields near the North Pole, an image she vaguely recalled from a TV movie. So, she grudgingly agreed to the move.

Just as she was getting used to the idea of moving, her parents had told her something else, much worse. They were going to take in a foster child, and this time she had no say in the matter. She raged and cried and asked why, but they wouldn't give her a satisfactory answer. She had been fuming ever since.

When Mom and Dad had seen how upset she was, they were contrite. Mom laid her hand on Katie's cheek. "Maybe we should have asked your opinion. You know we always try to take your feelings into consideration."

"So why not this time?" Katie demanded. Then Mom told the story of Siggi.

Siggi was the six-year-old son of a single mother. He had never known his father, who left the family when Siggi was a baby, then was killed in an accident when the boy was two years old. Siggi and his mother had lived in North Dakota until last year when she had become seriously ill. They moved back to Winnipeg where she'd grown up because, she said, she wanted to die at home.

Late one night last winter, when the wind was howling down the fireplace chimney of their house in Thunder Bay, the telephone had rung. Katie remembered the shock of that nighttime call. She was still awake, feeling drowsy in her warm bed. She could only hear part of what Mom was saying, "... so sorry... anything I can do to help." Katie had drifted off and in the morning, Mom brushed off her questions.

Katie knew now that that phone call had been from Siggi's mother. She was sick with worry over what was going to happen to her little boy when she died. Her only relative was a second cousin in Omaha who didn't want a thing to do with him.

Shortly after that call, Katie's parents told her that Mom was going to a geology conference in Winnipeg, but that was not true. She had really gone to see Siggi's mother. They had talked to a social worker and everything was arranged.

Six months later, just as they were preparing to leave Thunder Bay, Siggi's mother died and the little boy was moved into a temporary foster home. Temporary, because Mom and Dad had agreed to be his permanent foster parents. When they got to Winnipeg, they would pick him up and take him to the Yukon with them. "We won't apply for a formal adoption until you're ready for that move," said Dad. That'll be never, Katie thought.

"Why?" Katie had asked after she'd sat through the story of Siggi. "Why do we have to take this kid with us? Why can't he stay in the foster home in Winnipeg?"

"Katie Coll," said Mom. She was pleading. "He's just a little boy and he has no one."

"He has a foster family."

"But, they're strangers."

"Aren't we strangers?" asked Katie, trying to be reasonable. "I never heard of this kid before. Were you and his mother such good friends or something?"

She was genuinely trying to understand. Nothing Mom said made sense.

"Well, not really." Mom sat down beside her on the couch. She stared at her hands in her lap. She rubbed them together as if they were cold. "But, I did know her great-grandfather. He and I were good friends—a long time ago, long before you were born."

This story got more and more unbelievable. "An old man?" said Katie. "How come you were friends with an old man?"

"First of all, he wasn't old then," blurted Mom. She looked toward Dad who shook his head, almost imperceptibly. Suddenly she stopped. A tremor passed through her. Then she spoke again. "Katie Coll, we have so much and Siggi has nothing. He has no one. I know it's hard. I know we haven't handled this very well. But don't you think you could find it in your heart to welcome him into the family?"

Katie didn't speak for a long moment. Silence hung between them making the air seem heavy. Dad was sitting in his chair, leaning toward them. He had obviously decided to let Mom handle this one.

Katie thought of an argument. "You want me to say it's all right that some strange kid comes into our family. But it doesn't make sense. Remember when I was little you told me there were people who went without food because they couldn't afford to buy it? So we gave food to the food bank. We didn't invite them all home for supper."

She stopped, pleased with herself, hoping they would see she had logic on her side. But Mom didn't say anything. She folded her arms over her chest, and walked to the window that overlooked their backyard. She stood there, looking out at the clothes flapping on the line. Katie could see the ridges of Mom's shoulder blades on the back of her shirt.

When Mom turned toward her, there were tears in her eyes

and her voice was tight. "I'm sorry you feel this way, Katie. I can't explain just now but it's very important to me that we help Siggi. I hope you join your dad and me in welcoming him to the family."

That was that. And now, the day she'd been dreading had arrived.

──Chapter 2──
The Kid

They checked out of the fancy Winnipeg motel and drove to Polo Park Shopping Centre to pick up a few things for The Kid. That's how Katie thought of him now. The Kid.

They looked for things to keep a six-year-old occupied in the car on their long journey to the Yukon—markers, drawing paper, puzzles, books, and some little cars with doors and trunks that opened and shut.

"Do you think he'd prefer a race car or a truck?" Mom asked Katie.

"As if anybody cares what I think," said Katie, sulking.

Mom and Dad looked at each other and sighed. Katie knew how she was hurting them, but she wanted them to see her awful sense of betrayal. She still couldn't believe that her beloved parents, who had always, until now, respected her feelings and opinions, had made this momentous decision without her, with no regard for how she felt. How could they? Why? They mustn't respect her after all.

They drove the few blocks from the mall to the foster parents' house. Mom, with Katie beside her, drove her old brown Mazda into the lane behind the house, followed by Dad in their shiny-new black truck. Katie said, "I'll wait here in the car." She folded her arms across her chest.

"You have to come with us, Katie Coll," Mom said.

The three of them walked in a single file up the narrow back-yard walkway, past neat rows of vegetables on one side and a perfect patch of lawn on the other. The back of the house was cracked stucco. The door was green. A faint paint smell hung in the heavy air.

Dad knocked. The three of them huddled together on the doorstep. Dad had both his canes in one hand; with the free one he took Mom's hand and gave it a quick little squeeze, then dropped it as someone opened the door. A middle-aged woman in a shiny blue dress peered at them, not smiling. "I'm Mrs. Fielding," she said. "You must be Marc, Maggie, and Katie McKay." Then, "You're late." The blue dress looked stiff, as if it could stand up by itself.

Mom looked a little flustered. "I'm sorry," she said. "I guess it took a little longer than we thought to find the address."

"Come in. This is where you wipe your feet. It should be obvious that's what the mat is for. Goodness knows why I'm always having to point it out." The three of them wiped their feet carefully, not looking at each other.

Mrs. Fielding wore her grey hair in a precise, short cut. She didn't smile. She led the way through a tiny spotless kitchen to a tiny spotless living room. A woman rose from the couch and Mom greeted her warmly. Katie guessed that this was the social worker Mom had met last winter. Without really listening, Katie heard a jumble of introductions.

Katie's eyes swept the room, then focussed on the plastic-covered couch. A skinny little boy with white-blonde hair and almost invisible eyelashes was staring back at her. He was wearing pressed cotton pants and a short-sleeved buttoned-up shirt that still had fold marks from the package it had come in. She could see the comb lines in his pale wet hair. He looks like a nerd, she thought.

When she looked into his round blue eyes, she saw fear and confusion. She caught herself, on the verge of feeling sorry for him.
It's okay to hate him, she said in her mind. He's got no business
in our family.

The social worker introduced Siggi to Katie and Dad. Katie
turned away from him and looked out the window while Dad
shook his hand. Mom sat on the couch beside him. "Mrs. Fielding," asked the social worker, "will you show us your wonderful
garden?" And before anyone realized what was happening, she
was shooing Katie, Dad, and Mrs. Fielding toward the back door,
leaving Mom and Siggi alone.

Katie heard Mom say, "Siggi, do you remember the monkey at
the zoo spitting seeds out the side of its mouth while it watched
you eating that ice cream?" She laughed that soft laugh that came
so spontaneously when she talked about something special.

Katie didn't hear Siggi's answer because the door shut behind
her. The zoo! Katie had never been to a really big zoo in her life
and last winter Mom had taken The Kid to the Winnipeg Zoo and
hadn't even mentioned it!

Dad tried to take Katie's hand, but she jerked it away. She was
immediately sorry for her rudeness and slipped her hand into his.
"How about riding with Siggi in the backseat of the truck for a
while?" he asked quietly while the social worker oohed and aahed
over the climbing peas and Mrs. Fielding looked pleased and
proud. Katie turned away from Dad and walked down the alley a
little way, scuffing her running shoes in the dust. Then she went
back to the truck and stood beside it. "I'd rather not ride with
him," she said finally.

They loaded Siggi's stuff into the trunk of Mom's car. He had
a suitcase with all his clothes, a cardboard box full of toys, and

a backpack that he took in the car with him. Not much stuff, thought Katie. She was thinking of all the boxes that had come out of her room in Thunder Bay, all loaded into the cavernous moving van that, right now, was on the road to Whitehorse. She realized suddenly that at this moment she had no home. Everything stinks, she thought.

The Kid kept staring at Dad, at his canes and the way he walked on his artificial legs. He poked his head inside the truck to get a look at the special controls Dad needed to drive.

"He's just curious," Dad said quietly to Katie. She knew Dad usually felt annoyed when someone stared. Then he turned to Siggi. "I had an accident when I was a little older than you. But it's okay. I'm used to it."

Katie caught the little boy's eye. "Siggi. What kind of name is that?" she asked. Her tone made it sound like, what kind of dumb name is that?

"Icelandic," said Siggi, defiantly.

"Some of Siggi's ancestors came to Manitoba from Iceland, a long time ago," explained Mom. "His mother wanted him to remember his heritage, so she gave him an Icelandic name." She smiled, holding the car door for the little boy.

Siggi looked like he didn't care when he said good-bye to the woman who'd been his foster mother for weeks. Mrs. Fielding waved stiffly at him as the Mazda pulled away.

Then, unsmiling, she turned to Katie's open window as the truck throbbed to life and said, "You're a lucky young lady to get a ready-made brother."

— Chapter 3 —
On the Road

They left Winnipeg behind; a straight road stretched ahead to the edge of the world. Whitehorse was about 3,500 kilometres away. Dad said it might take about five days to get there, depending on how many stops they made. Heat shimmered from the highway in the hot prairie sun. Katie rode high in the truck with Dad. Her backpack lay on the floor between her feet. She read so she wouldn't have to talk. Dad, however, refused to take the hint. He wanted to talk about Siggi. He said that he and Mom wanted Siggi, and that Katie's attitude disappointed them both. If Katie would act like her old generous self toward the boy, they'd all be happy. Katie kept her eyes glued to her book and refused to answer. Finally he sighed heavily and stopped talking.

Mom followed in the Mazda with Siggi beside her. Once, she almost caught up with them. Katie turned to look through the rear window. She couldn't see much of Siggi because he was too short. She could see Mom though. Mom's head was constantly moving. There was the pale oval of her face as she looked at the road, then the quick dip sideways. She was talking—talking to The Kid. She was smiling.

That first night they tried to get a room with two beds plus a cot or a pullout couch, but they had to take two adjoining rooms. That meant The Kid got his own room with his own bathroom and television. Something woke Katie in the night. At first she thought the clock radio was still on. A low whining sound filled the room. A moment later, she realized the sound was coming through the wall. Siggi was crying.

Mom snapped on the bedside light as she got out of bed and pulled on her robe. "You two go back to sleep," she whispered as she turned off the light. Katie heard the door click shut, then a moment later, Mom's comforting voice through the thin wall. There was only one clear sentence when Siggi's voice rose to a wail. "I want my own mom!"

The second night they stopped at a motel with a pool. Siggi stared at Dad who was sitting on the edge of the pool, removing his artificial legs. But after Dad swam a couple of lengths, using his muscular arms and shoulders to propel himself through the water, the boy stopped staring and dog-paddled back and forth across the shallow end.

For the first time since they'd begun this endless trip, Katie felt something besides her misery. Her arms and legs had stiffened from long days in the car. Now they stretched into life as her body slipped through the cool, silky water. She quit thinking about anything except her strokes. She swam like someone obsessed, from end to end, over and over, touching, somersaulting, gliding, swimming.

When she came out, panting a little, Siggi was standing near the edge of the pool, a thin little boy in baggy trunks, his legs like sticks. Mom and Dad were in the hot tub, far enough away so that the sound of their voices carried, but not the words.

Katie looked down at Siggi. She looked into his pale round eyes and saw tears.

A little jab of pity prodded the edge of her mind. She was beginning to get used to squelching this feeling.

"What happened to my dog, Skippy?" He leaned toward her anxiously.

"I don't know," she answered. "Look. You're lucky we're taking you in. You can't ask us to take your stupid pet, too."

Siggi's expression hardened. "You're horrible," he said. "And mean."

She stiffened, not sure how to respond. She had never thought of herself as being mean. Before she could react, Siggi ran at her, head down. She took the blow in her stomach, and the next moment she was in the pool, shouting her rage between gasps and splutters, and Mom was running toward them while Dad was scrambling for his legs.

"No matter what anybody says," Katie shouted at Mom when she caught her breath, "he'll never be my brother. Never!"

It was about the middle of Alberta, when she'd finished reading her book, that Mom gave her the book on Victorian England.

"It's something that means a lot to me. I've had it since I was a little older than you, when I saved my allowance to buy it. I had a friend who was English and I wanted to learn all I could about life in his country. It's got a picture of a girl riding a horse, which I know you'll like. I've kept the book with me all these years. Now I want you to have it."

With the book came a metallic board and magnetized figures of a Victorian family: a father, a mother, a girl about Katie's age, a younger boy, and a small child who could have been either boy or girl because, as the book explained, toddlers of both genders wore dresses in those times, and boys didn't get their first haircut until they were five or six years old.

With the figures came a plastic bag full of magnetic costumes that stuck to the figures. Katie could dress the magnet family and change its clothes.

At first, Katie was annoyed with the gift. It had been years since she'd played with paper dolls, and she felt insulted. She wasn't a little kid! But she understood it was important to her mom so she decided to give it a chance. When she began reading the book, she realized it wasn't for children. It gave detailed information on the sixty-odd years that Queen Victoria had reigned over the British Empire. It told how, over those years, fashions had changed as the world had changed. The fashions in the bag were selected from the late Victorian era, around 1880 to 1900.

So Katie learned about stays and corsets. She became fascinated with spats and puffed sleeves. She stared at the girl with a long skirt riding on a black horse and imagined herself riding with her on her big black stallion. As the long days passed, she spent more and more time learning about the Victorians. She read of petticoats and camisoles, of bustles and bathing costumes made of heavy wool that covered most of the body. As she dressed the figures on the board, layering elaborate costumes over elaborate underclothing, she wondered what it would feel like to dress like this.

In the book, the girl was called Samantha and she was thirteen years old. She had started wearing her first real corsets. Until now she had worn something soft taking the place of a corset, called a vest.

Katie spent hour after hour delving into the details of the book. When Dad asked her what interested her most, she answered, "Everything." But if she'd answered absolutely truthfully, she would have said that what fascinated her most was this family. With permanent smiles painted on their faces, Katie imagined they lived perfect, happy lives. These parents wouldn't sacrifice their daughter's happiness for the sake of a... a nasty little kid who insulted her!

All these long days on the road, when she let herself think about what was happening in her life, she'd been asking herself the same questions. Why hadn't her parents discussed with her their plans to take Siggi into the family? Why did they feel they had to do this thing no matter what she thought?

When she asked Dad, he said, "You know your mom was an orphan, so she can't turn away from a boy who has lost both parents." But Katie knew the world was full of orphans and Mom had never before suggested they should take one into their family.

They developed a routine of Katie riding with one parent, Siggi with the other. Katie was riding with Mom northwest of Edmonton when they saw the mountains and a bear almost simultaneously. The black bear ambled out of the forest, shook his head and sniffed the wind, then turned and disappeared in the trees. Katie shivered, partly from fear of its wildness, partly in awe. The mountains were rugged—she had never seen anything so massive. Their tops, white with snow even in the heat of summer, were so high they pierced the clouds. The highway skirted several lakes. When the windows were down, the air was sharp and clean. They were driving into a different world, wilder, closer to nature.

The road climbed into the mountains. The highway was narrow in places and it twisted and curved up and up. They couldn't drive as fast as they had on the straight prairie roads. Occasionally they saw mountain sheep. In spite of her decision to hate everything about the move, Katie felt excited by the new landscape.

In northern BC they stayed in a log hotel in a place called Liard because they wanted to try the hot springs. They changed into their bathing suits, wrapped their towels around them, and walked across the highway and through the forest on a wooden sidewalk to the springs. There were signs warning of bears.

Several people were scattered here and there in pools among some trees. At first Katie thought the water would scald her, but when she got used to it, it felt wonderful. "You should come here in the wintertime—it's magic," a woman told her. "The vapour from the hot water condenses in the cold air. It's like swimming in a cloud."

Magic, thought Katie. But she kept her enjoyment of the new landscape to herself. She didn't want her parents to think she had found anything she liked in this new life they were foisting on her.

— Chapter 4 —
Yukon Territory

They reached Whitehorse on a hot summer afternoon of the sixth day of their journey from Winnipeg. While Katie was relieved that all the driving was coming to an end, she still wasn't happy to have left Thunder Bay. Yet, she was curious. She stared out the car windows at her new city. A few of the wooden buildings had false fronts like the ones in western movies. The downtown was built into a curve of the Yukon River and in the background were mountains. Mom and Dad found rooms at an ordinary motel. They left the Mazda there and all four of them climbed into the truck. Katie sat in the backseat with Siggi. She was so busy looking out the window, she forgot to be annoyed with him.

Dad drove them to a large, modern tourist bureau where they picked up a city map, then set off to find the home of the real estate agent who would show them the way to their new house. He turned into a neat suburban street and pulled up in front of a two-storey house that could have been in a new subdivision in Thunder Bay with its large front lawn and flowers growing by the double driveway. Mom went to the door and in a few minutes a woman came from the house, waved to them, got into a white pickup truck, backed out of the driveway, and accelerated down the street. "Her name's Betty," Mom told them.

It was soon obvious that Betty was taking them on the scenic tour. First they drove past a modern, industrial-looking complex. Mom said, "That's the Canada Games Building with all the sports facilities any of us could ever want, including a pool." They drove beside the mighty Yukon River, its beauty set off by those mountains in the background. Katie saw a tram filled with riders. "Look, Dad," she said, pointing.

"I see it," said Dad. "This is a tourist town after all."

"Whitehorse is nicer than I thought. It's a beautiful city," said Katie. "I'm glad you brought us here, Dad." She had also forgotten, momentarily, her anger at the move.

"Thanks, sweetheart." This was all Dad said, but Katie knew her approval was important to him. Mom was smiling.

The little procession left Whitehorse and continued down a highway with the mountains in the distance. They passed laundromats and service stations. They turned off the highway onto a narrow road where they glimpsed cabins through scrubby trees. The white pickup turned into a lane. The black truck followed and both vehicles came to a stop in front of a shabby log building. Some rusting pieces of old machinery littered the dusty yard. There was no grass, but here and there were clumps of weeds.

Mom and Dad got out of the truck and stood mutely together, staring at the shack. Betty bustled up to the door, keys in hand.

"Just a minute. There must be a mistake," said Mom, finding her voice. "This isn't a house. It's a little old log cabin."

"Mistake? I don't think so. You asked for a three-bedroom in the country where you could keep a horse. The next-door neighbour has a barn. Properties in the Whitehorse area have sold like hotcakes this summer. Everyone wants to get settled before the new school term. This is the only building available that suits your needs."

"Needs," said Dad dryly. "Is that an outhouse?" He raised a cane and pointed with the tip to a small log building back in the trees.

"Perhaps it's a little primitive," Betty conceded, "but we assumed from your email that you wanted the romantic experience of living in a log cabin in the North."

"Romantic?" said Mom sarcastically. "Does it have central heating?" Her voice changed and got harder. "I don't think this will do at all. My husband needs a proper bathroom. We all need a proper bathroom."

"Oh dear," said Betty. "I'm afraid there's been a misunderstanding. I thought you wanted a place where you could keep a horse."

"We do!" said Katie loudly, before Mom or Dad could say more.

"Such a fine place for children and pets," said Betty, smiling broadly at Katie.

"Pets!" said Siggi. "Can I have a dog?"

"Oh, a perfect place for dogs!" said Betty happily. "Dogs are important animals in the North. Everyone here has a dog."

"I once lived like this," said Dad wistfully. "I had a job out in the bush and we cooked on a wood stove. An outhouse would have been considered a luxury there!"

"There's nothing as cozy on a winter night as a wood fire," said Betty enthusiastically.

"This is crazy," said Mom, glaring at Dad. "You can't split wood," she said.

"I can," said Katie, thinking of the stable right next door. "And The Kid can learn. I mean, Siggi can learn."

"I'll chop wood," said Siggi.

"I think I'm getting soft in the head," said Mom, looking from Katie to Siggi and sighing, "but we may as well see the inside."

The cabin had the hot, stale smell of a building that had been closed for a long time. Betty left the door wide open. Some flies buzzed in the heat.

"This cabin was originally one huge room," she told them. "It's been fully insulated so the log walls are hidden under wallboard. And, it's recently been redecorated," she enthused, pointing at the bright robin's-egg-blue walls and the cheap vinyl on the floors.

"The stove in the middle keeps everything toasty warm, and is so romantic on a winter night," Betty gushed. Apparently she considered anything romantic a selling point. "The previous tenant wanted bedrooms, so voila! A few partitions, and there are three bedrooms. The two across the back are only six feet deep, but each is ten feet long! And the one off the kitchen area is even larger!"

"We could never get all our furniture in here," said Mom, looking around. There were a few kitchen cupboards in a corner of the main room, and attached to the wall was a chipped white sink. A large Husky Oil can stood under an open drain beneath the sink. "That blue colour is ghastly! Running water?" Mom asked in the same breath.

"You can get it delivered by truck. Very convenient," said Betty.

"We have to have a shower," said Mom, her voice sounding weak.

"There are public showers all over the place. There's one down the road at an RV Park. Very reasonable," said Betty. "And you probably noticed the laundromats on the way out here."

Dad was looking around. "Where could I have my office? I need room for a desk and computer."

"I'm sorry you don't like it," said Betty coldly as if they had just said something that offended her. "I'm sure something more to your liking could come available by spring, but right now, this is really the only option." She checked a notebook. "There is a one-bedroom in town. It's all I have left right now."

That evening, in their motel, the family had a rather heated discussion. By bedtime Mom had forgiven Dad for not asking for a picture of the property, and they had made a group decision. The cabin, with all its drawbacks, was better than a motel or a one-bedroom apartment. They would stay in it until something better came along.

"Yippee! I can get a dog!" shouted Siggi.

Mom and Dad smiled at each other over Siggi's head. Katie bit her tongue and clenched her fists until she felt her fingernails digging into her palms. Her only consolation was the possibility of a horse.

The next days were busy ones. Dad borrowed an old beat-up pickup truck from a geologist he'd be working with, and the whole family set out to clean the cabin's yard.

Mom picked up a rusty, twisted bicycle and carried it to the pickup. Dad stood without his canes, balancing his body with one shoulder against the truck box. He took the bike from Mom and heaved it over the side of the box with one powerful arm.

Katie saw her parents smile at each other. It made her feel homesick. She longed for the days that seemed long gone now, when they were in their real home and the three of them did things together and everything was as it should be. She sighed and went back to work.

She had already half-filled a bucket with small junk from the yard—rusted can lids and bits of plastic and Styrofoam coffee cups. She bent to pick up some rusty nails when her eye caught the glitter of a piece of broken glass, then another and another. Someone must have been breaking bottles here, or maybe using them for target practice. Some of the shards were thick brown beer-bottle glass, while other were clear and heavy, like pieces of pop bottles.

She had just straightened up when something hit her from behind and she went down. Her hands splayed out against the ground. Through the thick fog of shock, she felt a sharp pain in her right hand.

She got shakily to her feet and, in a daze, raised her hurt hand in front of her. She pulled a small piece of glass from the heel of her thumb and the blood dribbled down onto her wrist. When she saw the blood, she roared.

Mom and Dad turned from the truck in surprise.

"Look what he's done!" Katie shouted. "He's trying to kill me!"

She looked down then and saw the ragged hole in the knee of her jeans, and the scraped knee looking sore and raw. Her knee was still numb, but the sight of it through her torn pants was more than she could bear, and she began to cry.

Mom turned to Siggi. She looked upset. Katie could see his fear. She felt some satisfaction and cried a little louder.

"I'm sorry," said Siggi. "I was trying to pick this up." He pointed to an old tree stump lying uprooted among the stubbly weeds. "It was too heavy and I fell backwards against her."

"That's a lie!" shouted Katie. "He knocked me down. On purpose."

Mom looked from one to the other. Katie could see the emotions flickering across her face, which finally settled into an exasperated glare.

"Now, why would he want to do that, Katie?" she said. "Stop that silly sniffling. You're bigger than he is and should know better! I put the first aid kit in the cabin. Come with me so I can look after those scratches."

Katie was shocked out of her tears. Her mother had never talked that way to her before. As she followed Mom to the cabin, she turned and saw Siggi struggling to pick up an old hubcap for Dad to throw into the truck box. He was squatting in the dust, watching her out of scrunched-up eyes. It was hard to tell from this distance, but she could have sworn he was grinning. Katie glumly followed Mom into the cabin. After Mom cleaned the wound and bandaged it, Katie went back to the yard. She wouldn't acknowledge Siggi, not even by looking at him.

After the yard was cleaned, they set to work inside the house. Mom had asked the landlord to paint the place. The landlord said it had been painted just last year, but if she wanted to do the work, he would supply the paint. So Mom chose soft, buttery yellow for all the walls, and white for the ceilings and trim. "The yellow looked like a wash of spring sunshine," she said. "We'll appreciate that in the dark days of winter." They drove from the motel early each morning to work at making their new home livable.

Katie worked long hours painting her room. Siggi ran a few errands, then was told to play outside. Katie couldn't understand why she had to work so hard and he didn't. She got tired of Mom and Dad saying, "He's just a little boy."

Mom and Dad were excited when the big moving van rolled into the yard, but Katie felt discouraged. She'd been hoping beyond hope that she'd wake up and find the move was only a bad dream. When she saw her Thunder Bay belongings being carried into their Yukon cabin, her last hope was dashed.

Mom and Dad supervised as the movers carried in beds, dressers, table and chairs, couch, TV, DVD player, Dad's desk and computer. Boxes of dishes, bedding, and clothes were piled in the main room. The moving men carried in the easy chairs, then carried them out again when Dad said there was no room for them. Dozens of boxes had to be left on the truck. Along with the surplus furniture, they would go into storage in Whitehorse until a bigger house became available.

Mom hung up her collection of Mexican blankets in their kitchen/living room. Their bright colours looked striking against the soft yellow walls. Katie used to like the blankets, but now they seemed annoyingly cheerful. They only emphasized how unhappy she felt. She hated this cabin and everything about it. Her mom and dad hadn't said another word about a horse. She was beginning to think they just said that to get her to co-operate.

Feeling lonely and shut out, Katie spent every spare minute in her miniature room with her miniature Victorian doll family. There was no space in her room for a chair, so she sat on her narrow bed with the book propped on her knees. In one picture the Victorian family was eating an elaborate picnic spread on a snowy cloth on a clipped lawn beside a pond in a park. People strolled indolently by, their broad-brimmed hats shading their eyes from the summer sun.

On another page, the family was gathered round a blazing fireplace in a richly decorated but cluttered room. The mother was at an easel, painting a portrait of her family. The toddler was at her feet playing with spools on a string. The father sat in a wingback chair, reading aloud from a large red book. The young boy was stretched out on the rug in front of the blazing hearth, his chin on his hands, gazing at his father in adoration.

It was the girl, Samantha, leaning against the back of her father's chair and reading over his shoulder, who interested Katie most. She felt as if she was getting to know the girl. When she was alone, Katie was falling into the habit of talking to Samantha as she would to a real friend. She imagined Samantha answering with an English accent. Samantha said that she understood how Katie must feel. She said she felt bad for her, and that Katie had every right to feel hard-done-by. Samantha was the only one who understood.

—Chapter 5—
Two Birthday Presents

School was starting on Tuesday and Katie's twelfth birthday was coming up on Saturday. It was going to be the worst birthday of her life. The only thing that could save it would be if Dad carried through with his hint that a horse was in her future.

On the first day of school, Katie and Siggi waited at the end of the lane for the school bus. Mom walked out with them and when the bus arrived, she got on and introduced herself and the children to the bus driver.

"Are you going to be okay?" she asked Katie and Siggi. She had taken them to "Meet the Teacher" last evening, but today she couldn't go with them. It was her first day of work.

Katie nodded, anxious for her mother to leave. She was embarrassed to be treated like a baby so she hurried to find an empty seat. Siggi was still with Mom at the front of the bus. Mom took his hand and led him to Katie's seat, told him to sit there, then she hurried away, thanked the driver, and ran down the steps.

As they pulled past the lane, Katie waved, but Siggi refused to look out the window. His face was solemn and even more pale than usual. Mom had wet his blonde hair and carefully combed it back from his face. It had dried now and was falling across his eyes. He sat very still, then looked down, staring at his new jeans and sneakers.

At school, Siggi disappeared into the entrance of the elementary wing. Katie said good-bye, but he stared straight ahead and didn't answer. She thought that he looked kind of pathetic walking past all those yelling kids on the playground. Katie walked around the building to the entrance for higher grades.

Katie's homeroom teacher, Mme. Legault, asked her to sit with three girls so they could take turns editing each other's work. One of them Katie recognized from the bus. She was tall and strong-looking. She had a wide cheerful face with shining brown eyes and long, straight, black hair. Katie felt plain beside her, with her mousy hair and thin face. She usually felt insignificant around bigger more vibrant people because she was short and small-boned.

The girl's name was Madeleine. "Everyone calls me Mad," she said with a smile. "But don't worry, I'm usually pretty even-tempered."

Katie laughed, looked into Mad's brown eyes, and relaxed. She saw nothing there but uncomplicated good humour. Within minutes they had shared their life stories, and Katie found out that Mad lived down the road from her. Mad introduced Katie to Sara and Meredith and, after working happily together through the morning, the four of them ate lunch together. Mad promised to save a seat for Katie on the bus on the way home. Katie forgot to be miserable. She even forgot about Siggi.

Katie and Mad were chatting on the bus like old friends when out of the corner of her eye Katie saw Siggi getting on. He stopped by her seat, confused, then went toward the back of the bus. From where she was sitting she couldn't see who he was sitting with. She felt a little stab of guilt, then forgot him again when Mad asked her about her friends in Thunder Bay.

At supper, Katie went on and on about Mad and Sara and Meredith.

When her parents turned to Siggi to ask about his day, he just shoveled pasta into his mouth and didn't answer. As soon as his plate was empty, he asked to be excused. As she nibbled at her fruit crisp, Katie could see him out the window. He was kicking stones into a puddle, his hands plunged into his pockets, more like an old man trying to fill the hours of the day than a little boy with things to do. Mom excused herself and went outside. Katie could see them talking, then Mom leaned over and hugged him. Her face was sad.

She came in, leaving the boy alone. "Some of the older children on the bus were picking on Siggi," Mom said, looking at Katie. "He's too little to know how to handle it. Katie, I want you to promise you'll sit with him on the school bus every day."

"But Mom," Katie protested.

"Not another word, Katie. Your responsibility is to take care of Siggi, at least until he's made friends and things have sorted themselves out."

"And it doesn't matter whether I make friends or not. All that matters is that... that kid!" Katie muttered through gritted teeth.

"Katie, I'm surprised at you!" said Dad. "I think you should go to your room until you cool down."

The next morning, when Katie and Siggi got on the bus, Mad was saving a seat for her. "Sorry, I've got to sit with him," said Katie nodding toward Siggi.

"Okay," said Mad cheerfully. Katie sat with Siggi a couple of rows back. A boy stopped by Mad's seat, screwed up his face and said "Phew, something smells bad—must be one of them dirty injuns." Mad looked at him defiantly but didn't respond. Katie knew his behaviour was racist; she had heard similar cruelties in her old school in Thunder Bay. Mom and Dad had encouraged her to confront such injustices, but she couldn't think of anything she could do to change things, so she decided not to get involved. Mad moved to sit with another girl and Katie could only watch as the two of them talked and laughed all the way to school.

Saturday—Katie's birthday—finally came. At breakfast there was a pretty blue parcel beside her plate. It was small and tied with a silver ribbon. Inside was a velvet-lined box containing a silver locket. Inside the locket was a picture of Katie and her parents taken last summer on the shore of Lake Superior. "It's nice," was all Katie could manage to say. She had hoped against hope that she would finally get a horse for her birthday. She was disappointed, even with a beautiful piece of jewelry like the locket.

There was a note in the card from Mom telling Katie how sorry she was that Katie was having a hard time getting used to the changes in her life. Only the last line spoiled everything. "This picture will have to do until we get one with all four of us." Katie put the locket around her neck and put her hand over it, feeling the smooth, cool metal. It really was beautiful. She vowed she would keep this locket forever, and never, never would she allow anyone to change the picture.

"Everybody into the truck. We've got a surprise," said Dad after breakfast. Katie's heart skipped a beat.

They drove down the dirt road that ran past their lane. About half a kilometre down the road was a gateway with a sign arched over it, saying, "Haggarty's Ranch." The letters were burned into the wood like a brand. Katie was getting more and more excited. Maybe her wishes were coming true at last.

They bumped up a long winding lane past some spruce trees. At the end of the lane was a log cabin and behind the cabin was a low log building. The owner of the place, Mr. Haggarty, came out of the cabin when they pulled up. He was wearing jeans and a Blue Jays cap pulled down on his forehead.

The family followed him to the building behind the cabin. A heap of manure was piled by the door. Off to the side was a log corral.

Mr. Haggarty took off his cap and scratched the top of his bald head with the same hand, then pulled on the hat again. "So this is the young lady. You don't look too strong to me."

"I'm stronger than I look," said Katie.

"Maybe we should see the birthday gift," said Mom.

"Wait here," the man said. Katie bit her cheek to help her stay calm. She conjured up her vision of riding a powerful black stallion across the frozen fields that stretched to the North Pole. Well, there was no snow here and she had learned that Whitehorse was nowhere near the North Pole. But there was a big empty, grassy field behind the barn. She could ride her fire-breathing stallion there. She felt a little dizzy.

Mr. Haggarty rolled open a big sliding door and disappeared inside the dark cavern of the barn. The familiar, acid smell of horse manure wafted out to them, and Katie moved up and down on her toes. She heard the clop of horseshoes striking the floor of the barn before she saw anything. Then Mr. Haggarty appeared in the doorway, a rope in his hand.

What followed Mr. Haggarty out of the barn was not the powerful stallion of Katie's imagination. It was a squat pony, bigger than a Shetland, but smaller than a horse. It had a shaggy forelock of creamy hair covering its eyes and the same whitish-coloured mane and tail. Its body was grey, and its face and legs a darker grey, almost black.

Katie didn't speak for a moment. The pony was—she couldn't think of any other word—ugly. She couldn't see its eyes through the tangled forelock, and its legs were so short relative to its body that it looked stumpy.

"This here little mare's five years old," said Mr. Haggarty. "Icelandic horse. They call 'em horses in Iceland but most of us Canadians call 'em ponies 'cause of their height. Came to a horse show in Edmonton, and they couldn't take her back. Once a horse leaves Iceland it can never go back in case it brings in a disease that might infect their herds. This is a mighty old strain and they want to protect them over there. The Icelandic government doesn't allow any other kind of horse to be brought in, so this is the only kind in the whole country. I figured if these little horses are as hardy as they say in a place they call Iceland, they should be good in the Yukon, so I bought her."

"What's her name?" asked Katie. She parted the long forelock with her hands and gazed into big liquid black eyes. There was something mysterious way back in those eyes. They were full of understanding, too.

"I can't say it. Somethin' Icelandic. Somethin' like Valgrum-skirgrum… oh, heck, I can't remember. It had about fifty letters in it an' I couldn't make head nor tail of any of it. I figure she's yours now, so you'll think of a Canadian name for her."

"The deal is," Dad explained to Katie, "you help with the horses here for an hour every day. That'll help pay to board your pony."

"I don't usually do this," said Mr. Haggarty. "I've got six horses here. The old gelding belongs to me and the rest of 'em are boarders. Right now, I'm findin' it all a bit of a handful, so I told your dad if you're as handy as he says you are, I could use your help. You sure you're strong enough to clean out the barn?"

Before Katie could answer, Dad spoke up. "My parents have a tourist business on Prince Edward Island. They keep a few horses for trail rides. Katie's been helping them out for years now. Does a good job, too."

"What do you say?" asked Mom, smiling at Katie.

"Thank you," Katie forced herself to say, after a long embarrassing silence. She was deeply disappointed that her beautiful stallion in reality was only a homely pony. Mom held her hands for Katie to step onto so she could mount. There was no saddle yet. "Maybe next birthday," said Dad.

"You can let her have her head out there in the open," said Mr. Haggarty, pointing to the field behind the barn. A car horn sounded in the distance. Katie murmured in a low voice to reassure the pony, reaching forward to pat her thick, muscular neck.

The little horse snorted, seeming to dance as it started into the open field. Katie urged it to a trot, then encouraged it with hands and clicking tongue to move into a gallop. Expecting the bounce of the gallop, she was surprised that the pony moved into a different gait, very smooth and quite fast. Katie was able to ride erect, hardly feeling any up and down motion. It was almost like flying!

When she returned to the barnyard, Mom was in the corral leading an old black gelding around in wide circles. Siggi was perched on the horse's back, hanging onto its mane.

"Look at me," shouted Siggi. "I can ride, too! His name's Dan."

Katie refused to look at him. Mom reached her arm up and steadied him as he slid to the ground. Then everyone turned back to Katie.

Mr. Haggarty chuckled as she slipped from the pony's back.

"Didn't expect that gait, did ya? It's somethin' only these ponies can do. They tell me it's easier on people ridin' for miles and miles over those hills and rocks in Iceland."

Mr. Haggarty led the pony to the corral. "She seems well-behaved even though things here must seem strange with a different language and all."

Katie wondered what the mystery was in those calm liquid eyes.

Dad got his camera from the truck and asked Mom, Siggi, and Katie to smile. Katie scurried around to Mom's other side so she wouldn't have to stand beside The Kid for the picture. Then Dad handed the camera to Mr. Haggarty to snap another. "Let's get the four of us in front of the new pony," said Dad. "Then the birthday girl will be in a picture with both her Icelandic brother and her Icelandic pony." Katie didn't smile for this one.

Katie stayed at Haggarty's to work after the others left. Later, walking home, she realized that she had forgotten how miserable she was for a whole hour. Before grooming three of the horses, she'd used a curry comb to unsnarl her pony's long mane and tail, and brushed her coat until it shone.

Her pony. She hugged the thought to her. Maybe it was ugly, but it was her very own pony. At last. If only Mom and Dad would come to their senses and send The Kid away, maybe the Yukon wouldn't be such a bad place to live after all.

Even as she thought this, she realized her parents would never send Siggi away. They were trying to bribe her by giving her a pony.

Katie knew that she must be the one to get rid of The Kid if she wanted her old happy life back. The problem was that she had no idea how to make him disappear.

— Chapter 6 —
Magic Yukon

Over the next couple of months, life fell into a predictable routine. Katie exercised her pony every day after she cleaned the barn and groomed the horses. Siggi sabotaged Katie every chance he got. He habitually hid her library books until they were overdue. He denied everything. Mom said, "Now, why would he want to do a thing like that?" just as if Katie had made up the story.

Mad and her friends were friendly with Katie, but she didn't see them outside of school. She was sure that if she planned something, she'd have to cancel because Mom would tell her to look after The Kid. Sometimes she and Mad talked on the phone about homework, but Dad made her limit her calls to five minutes because he had to have quiet in the small cabin so he could concentrate on his data analysis. Once she invited Mad over for a sleepover and Mad said, "Your little brother will be there, right?" Katie felt her face getting hot. She said, "Oh, never mind," and hurried away.

So Katie continued to spend a lot of time in her room. She felt terribly lonely. Her best friend, the one she spent the most time with, was Samantha. The Victorian magnet-girl had become as real in Katie's mind as any girl at school. She was able to tell Samantha her troubles, confiding to the painted face her anger at her parents. She could imagine Samantha's sympathy. It was all very comforting.

Once when Katie was galloping her pony across the field in bright sunshine, she sensed that someone was riding beside her, enveloped in a cloud of fog. She pulled up at the end of the field. Through the haze, she could make out the wavering form of a horse and rider.

"What is the name of your horse?" a clear voice asked from the fog. It was a young girl's voice and the words were enunciated crisply, with an English accent. Katie knew it was Samantha. She was very excited but, strangely, not surprised.

"I haven't named her yet," she answered. "Nothing seems right."

"Mine is Jimbo," said Samantha. "He's just a hack. We keep him to pull a carriage, but I ride him sometimes."

"What's a hack?" asked Katie.

"Just an ordinary horse—nothing special."

Then, before Katie could say more, the fog began to whirl upward into the sky, like a whirlwind, and was gone.

"Samantha?" Katie called. "Samantha. Come back." Nothing was there but the silent, empty field. Her little horse shook its head, rattling its bridle. Katie was struck with that familiar feeling of loneliness and loss. Why couldn't she have a best friend like other girls did? Her chest felt constricted. But she refused to cry. Samantha was gone. Katie didn't know how to bring her back, so she drew her hand over her eyes, turned her pony, and galloped back to the barn.

Whenever she was out riding in the following weeks, she watched and hoped for Samantha to appear again. But the only time Katie felt her friend's presence was when she was able to imagine herself into the scenes of the Victorian book.

Siggi wasn't doing well at school. His teacher said he daydreamed too much. "She said he needs lots of attention from us," Mom told Katie and Dad when Siggi was out of earshot.

"He gets plenty of attention," responded Katie indignantly.

"Around here it's Siggi, Siggi, nothing but Siggi, morning, noon, and night."

Mom obviously didn't agree because, from that time on, every moment she could spare from her job and household duties she spent with the little boy.

One evening Mom sat with Siggi on the sofa and showed him a scrapbook his mother had made in those last sad months. Katie, reading nearby on the couch, sneaked a few peeks at the scrapbook. There were pictures of Siggi's mother from her babyhood and girlhood and a wedding picture—the only picture of Siggi's dad. One page was labeled "Descended from Noble Vikings." Underneath was a picture of a three- or four-year-old Siggi wearing a metal helmet with horns. It looked like a Halloween costume. Below that were some faded yellow snapshots of long-dead ancestors. There was one modern coloured picture in the book labeled "Northern Lights, Iceland." Katie registered snippits of what Mom was saying, "northern lights... beautiful... Iceland about as far north as the Yukon..."

Another page was labeled "Descended from the English—Lords of the Seas." Again there was a picture of little Siggi, this time in a rowboat with his mother. As on the other page, there were also some old yellow snapshots of relatives. Mom stared at these, particularly at a picture marked "Siggi's Great-Great Grandfather," until the boy impatiently reached out and turned the page. When Mom said it was time for her to get supper, he grabbed the scrapbook, hugged it to his chest, and ran off with it to his room.

Then there was the dog. One day Mom took Siggi into White-horse and they came home with a half-grown black-and-white mutt.

"Looks like it won't get too big," said Dad. "And short-haired is good. What do you want to call it, Son?"

Katie stiffened. The Kid isn't his son, she thought.

"Skippy," said Siggi. He dropped to his knees and hugged the little dog. Skippy wiggled all over, his tail flailing the air, his pink tongue licking salty tears from the boy's cheeks.

"Mind you put him on a leash every time you take him out," said Mom. "Remember what the lady said about wild dogs. We don't want him running loose and getting mixed up with them."

"Wild dogs?" asked Dad.

"It seems a lot of folks around here keep a few sled dogs for recreation. But, as anywhere else, some people are irresponsible. There's been a pack of wild dogs running lose. Someone reported that their goat had been killed by wolves a month or so ago, but this lady thinks it wasn't wolves, but dogs gone wild."

Katie shivered.

"I suppose the authorities will deal with them, but it doesn't pay to take chances," said Dad. "Promise to keep Skippy on a leash and to take good care of him?"

"I promise," said Siggi. "Can he sleep with me?"

"Well, maybe beside your bed," said Mom, glancing at Dad out of the corner of her eye and smiling. We'll cut down a box to make a nice bed for him."

Katie felt that strange mix of emotions that always came over her where Siggi was concerned. She knew she should be glad that he had something of his own to love, something that would love him in return. She knew how she should feel, but, again, she was angry. She had wanted a horse her whole life, but she had to wait until her twelfth birthday, and what she got wasn't even a real horse. Not only that, but she was expected to work to help pay the expenses. Siggi asked for a dog and he got a dog. Just like that.

It seemed that Mom and Dad couldn't do enough to try to make him happy. Why? she kept wondering. Why is he so important to them? Especially to Mom?

Winter came in early November. It was no colder than what they were used to in Thunder Bay and there was less snow. The days were shorter though, and darkness fell earlier and earlier each day. In the mornings, Katie and Siggi caught the bus in the black dark, and it was dark again when they came home in the afternoons.

One cold evening, when the snow was crystalline and crunchy underfoot, Katie bundled up and went outside after supper. It was her turn to fill the wood box. When she breathed the still, frosty air, it felt dry and hard inside her nose, like frozen metal. The air is dangerous, she thought. She knew she could damage the lining inside her nose, or, worse, her lungs, so she took shallow little breaths.

It seemed not as dark as usual at this time of day. She lifted her gaze upward and gasped. The sky was filled with stars, like diamonds spread on velvet. She had often seen the stars from the school bus or the cabin windows. But tonight, in the cold, they seemed magnified, hanging close to the earth. She felt that she could reach up and pluck them from the sky like apples from a tree.

Forgetting the wood, she ran inside and called the others. They pulled on parkas, mitts, and boots and came out with her to stare and be amazed.

Katie found the Big Dipper first, and from that she found Polaris, the North Star.

"I always get excited when I see it," said Mom. "I think it's because we Canadians are a northern people. It's our very own star."

Dad knew more about constellations than the rest of them. He balanced himself on one cane so he could point with the other to Cassiopeia, the big W. "Use the bottom right side of the W to find the Andromeda Galaxy," he said. "It's made up of billions of stars. Now look down to the right of Andromeda to find Pegasus, the flying horse."

"It doesn't look like a horse," said Siggi.

"I think I can make out a head and four legs," Katie said.

"You see horses everywhere," said Siggi. "You've got horses on the brain."

"I've seen a picture of Pegasus," said Katie, ignoring him. "A white horse with big fluffy wings. It was ridden by a Greek god named Bellerophon."

"It is a little hard to see," said Mom to Siggi. "I think the Greeks had better imaginations than we do."

Typical, thought Katie. Mom's taking his side. She grabbed an armload of wood then left them there. She went inside and quickly got ready for bed. She'd rather sleep than listen to them explaining constellations to the little brat.

As she drifted off, she thought of naming her pony Pegasus. But somehow the big winged steed that Bellerophon had ridden into so many battles didn't seem a good match for her little Icelandic pony.

She fell asleep almost immediately and dreamed of riding Pegasus in a big grassy field. She looked over her shoulder, past the mythical horse's big white rump, and there were Mom, Dad, and Siggi in the truck. Mom was leaning out the window and shouting something. At first Katie couldn't make out the words, but suddenly the meaning came to her. "Come back, Katie! Siggi needs the horse."

They wanted her horse! But it was hers! Her very own! She urged Pegasus into a gallop, and he galloped on and on, but every time she looked over her shoulder, the truck was closer. The horn was blaring and the three people inside were shouting at her. Suddenly, Siggi was running ahead of the truck. He was running faster than it could go.

Siggi ran alongside Pegasus. Just as he was reaching for the bridle, Katie could feel Pegasus bunching his powerful muscles, and suddenly they left the ground. They were flying!

Katie looked down, under the spreading white wing, down at the truck, which was stopped now in the field. Mom, Dad, and Siggi were standing near it, shouting and gesturing for her to come down.

Her eyes flew open. Her heart was beating hard. Mom was standing by the bed with a mug in her hand. Katie glanced at her clock radio. She couldn't have been asleep for more than a few moments.

"I'm sorry if I woke you, Katie Coll," Mom said. "I just made some hot chocolate, and I thought you might like some before you went to sleep."

"Oh, Mom," said Katie. Then, she couldn't help it. She started to cry. Mom put down the mug, reached for her, and she was in her mother's arms.

"Katie Coll," Mom murmured into her hair. "I'm sorry you're so unhappy."

Katie didn't answer. She snuggled down against Mom as she used to when she was a tiny child and had wakened, crying, from a bad dream.

Something snapped loudly, like a gunshot, and Katie jumped.

"Shh," said Mom. "It's just the frost in the log walls."

A wolf, or a dog, howled in the distance, long and mournfully. Katie closed her eyes. Her mind was full of giant stars, cracking frost, howling animals, and flying horses.

"The Yukon is a magic place, isn't it?" Katie whispered.

The cabin door banged. Siggi and Dad came in laughing, their happiness sounding clearly through the thin partition. Mom sprang to her feet.

"Is there a little boy out there who wants some hot chocolate?" she called. And she went to them, leaving Katie alone in her cramped little room.

—Chapter 7—
Wild Dogs

The family was sitting around the table late on a Sunday morning. The electric light shining from above made a circle of light in the darkness of late November. Katie was full, but Siggi was still eating pancakes—his third helping. Mom and Dad were working their way through their second pot of coffee while reading the Saturday Globe and Mail.

Katie spread her doll clothes on her side of the table. She was dressing Samantha and the others from the doll family for Sunday in the park. Samantha was wearing a split skirt. It had wide pant legs so she could be active, but when she walked, it looked as if she was wearing an ordinary skirt. Katie had learned that girls didn't wear pants in Victorian times unless they were disguised as more ladylike apparel.

"Any plans for the day?" Mom murmured to no one in particular.

"There's some reading I should catch up on," said Dad. "Why? Want to go for a drive?"

Mom yawned. "Reading sounds great. Even though I slept in, I'm still exhausted from last week. It's taking me a while to get used to this new job. How about you children?"

"I'm going to Haggarty's," said Katie suddenly, scooping her dolls into their box. "I hardly ever have enough time to ride as much as I'd like."

"What do you want to do, Son?" asked Dad.

Siggi hesitated for a moment, slowly licking maple syrup from his fork. His pale eyes darted to Katie, then back to Dad. Like a snake, Katie thought.

"I want to go riding, too," he said.

"We'll have to call Mr. Haggarty to see if we can take Dan out," said Mom. "If he says yes, I'll take you riding for an hour or so."

"I don't want to ride Dan. I want to ride the Icelandic pony." He was looking directly at Katie now. Challenging her.

Katie felt her face get hot. "Keep your slimy little toad hands off my horse," she said through clenched teeth. "She's mine. Nobody can ride her unless I say so."

"Katie!" Mom's tone was a mixture of shock and anger.

Dad was staring at Katie over his glasses as if he'd never seen her before. "I don't like who you're becoming," he said at last. "You used to be generous. Now you act thoughtless and spoiled. What's happening, Katie?"

Katie wanted to say that the pony was the only thing that was all hers, now that she had to share her parents. But when she looked at their shocked faces, she couldn't say it. She could see they were as upset as she was. They didn't understand because they didn't want to understand.

Katie jumped up and ran to her room. "Do what you want!" she shouted. "I don't have any say in what goes on around here any-way." She slammed the door behind her.

At first there was silence on the other side of her door, then she could hear her parents whispering. Silence again. Then a light rap on her door. She was lying on her bed, holding her breath, her chest heaving with suppressed sobs.

"Katie," Mom said softly, her voice carrying through the thin door, "we're going to Haggarty's. Will you come with us?"

"I'll go later." Katie tried to keep her voice calm, but it shook just a bit. "Don't worry. I'll do my work."

"If you're sure," said Mom. "But we'd enjoy ourselves more if you came with us."

Katie didn't answer. She heard them putting on their outdoor clothes and the cabin door opening and closing. Silence. They had left her. They didn't care about her one little bit. They were probably happy to be going off alone with that... that Kid!

They were gone until mid-afternoon. Katie was deeply immersed in the Victorian book when they came back. She had forgotten her anger for a few hours. But it came rushing back when Siggi announced, "I rode the horse." He looked at Katie defiantly.

She put away her book and went to the door. She pulled on her parka, not speaking.

"Mr. Haggarty was happy for us to give Dan some exercise," said Mom. She put her hand on Katie's shoulder. "Don't worry. We didn't touch your pony."

Katie shook off the hand. She could tell by Mom's tone that she still thought Katie was being unreasonable.

"We're ready for something hot to eat," said Dad. "Wouldn't you like to have a bite with us?"

"I'm not hungry," said Katie. She slammed out of the house, pulling on her mittens as she went. She hadn't told Dad that she'd eaten two apples and a cheese sandwich while they were out—but then, he hadn't asked.

The afternoon was dimly illuminated by pale wintry light. She jogged at the side of the road, avoiding ruts made before the ground froze, her boots crunching in the snow, her breath exploding in little clouds.

The cabin was dark at Haggarty's and the car was gone. She

often came when Mr. Haggarty was out, so she didn't worry. She went straight to the barn. The steamy warmth enveloped her as she rolled the barn door back just far enough to squeeze through. She pulled it shut behind her and snapped on the lights. Bare bulbs spaced along the ceiling shone dimly in the gloom.

Katie heard as much as she saw the horses welcoming her. Her pony, alone in a box stall, thrust its head over the wall, banging against the boards. Katie rummaged in her pocket and brought out a potato. She felt for the knife Mr. Haggarty kept on a shelf and cut the vegetable into pieces. She told her troubles to her pony as it crunched. It looked at her with those calm, accepting eyes and she felt herself relaxing.

Dan shuffled in his stall. Katie could hear his halter rope rubbing against the manger as he tested its strength.

The other horses were out. The various owners had more time for riding on weekends, so the stalls were often empty when Katie came on Saturday or Sunday. She didn't have as much work to do on these days since the owners had the time to groom their animals themselves.

Katie checked the mangers. Mr. Haggarty hadn't put the evening food out yet, so she would do it. There was a bin with a slanting lid at the back of the barn. She found the pail in it, and precisely measured a quantity of chopped grain for each manger, walking back and forth humming to herself. Next, she filled the water buckets from a trough next to the bin. She loved to be there when Mr. Haggarty filled the trough in the morning with a gasoline engine that putt-putt-putted as it pumped water from a well beneath the floor. She felt relaxed and happy here within this cozy little world.

Finished with her work, she bridled her pony and led it outside.

The winter light had almost disappeared and it would soon be as dark as night. She turned back to flick the switch to the yard light. She carefully rumbled the door closed behind them, then led the little mare to the woodpile illuminated by the strong light shining from high on a nearby pole.

She climbed a couple of steps upward on the wood, testing each foothold for stability before putting her weight on it. When she was high enough, she swung her leg over the pony's back. She wished she could just take hold of the mane and jump on, but learning to do that would have to wait until spring. Her bulky winter clothes made her movements too awkward for such gymnastics.

"Whoa," she murmured as she adjusted the scarf over her face. She had learned from experience that if she didn't cover her face well when she went for a ride, the sharp wind could freeze white patches on her cheeks and nose before she was aware of the cold.

She wished she had gone for her ride before her work in the barn. Now that it was almost dark, it would be dangerous to go for a gallop. She must hold her pony to a walk and trust the mare's instinct to keep her from stepping into a hole or walking into a fence.

Katie had ridden about halfway across the field when the pony heard something. It suddenly became alert, with head up and ears forward. It paused, listened a moment, gathered itself, then bolted. Katie pulled on the reins and struggled to regain her balance. Then she heard it.

The faint yapping of animals floated on the frosty air. The pony galloped even faster as the yapping pursued them. Katie was frightened because her pony was so frightened. She decided the safest course was to gallop back to the safety of the barn. She pulled hard on the left rein, trying to turn the little mare.

The sounds were getting louder and more frenzied. Katie looked hurriedly over her shoulder, and saw shadowy shapes against the snow, bounding toward them. She couldn't tell in the fading light if they were dogs or wolves. She had never heard such a wild cacophony of yelping before.

Katie was pulling on the one rein with all her strength, but the mare would have none of it. Every instinct was telling the little horse to flee from the attackers. She took the bit in her teeth and burst into an even faster gallop. Katie scrabbled for balance. She tightened her legs against the pony's sides and grasped a handful of mane. With the other hand she pulled hard on both reins to regain control, but the animals were getting closer and the pony kept the bit tight in her teeth.

In hasty glances over her shoulder, Katie saw an animal burst ahead of the pack. She saw the gleam of a fang as it nipped the pony's heel. The mare gathered her body into a concentrated ball of fury, then it kicked out. Katie started to slide sideways. Still clutching the mane, she righted herself with enormous effort. She felt the shudder of the hoofs connecting with something solid and heard a high-pitched yip. The pony exploded forward once again.

Katie could see clearly now. The moon had appeared and the field was bright. The hounds were still at the pony's heels. Katie changed tactics. Instead of trying to control her pony, she would encourage her horse to outrun those slathering animals. She leaned forward like a jockey, urging the pony on. Katie looked back. The animals were falling behind!

The little pony swung its head to look at its pursuers and Katie could see the white of its terrified eye. A dark shape had broken from the pack and was bounding ahead of the others, gradually pulling alongside. It was running faster than the pony. It sprang for the mare's head and fangs clamped on the sensitive nose.

The pony screamed with fear and pain. She reared, the hound hanging there. The mare shook her head as a dog shakes a rat, and the animal fell to the ground. The pony reared a second time and struck the fallen animal with both front feet, again and again, as Katie clung for dear life.

The rest of the pack was closing in. The horse, blood pouring from her wounded nose, leaped forward, whinnying a high note of pain and defiance. Katie had never ridden so fast and hard. The pony was literally running for her life. Katie knew their pursuers wouldn't be satisfied until they had pulled the brave little mare to the ground. Katie was terrified.

The pursuers were gaining. They were on both sides of the horse now. A big animal appeared on the left, ran ahead, bunched its body for the effort, and leaped. Katie thudded her boots against the pony's sides. Then the most wondrous thing happened.

Just as the big dog leaped for the pony's throat, Katie felt a shift in the mare's gait. The bone-shattering thuds suddenly ceased, and she was being carried along as if on a smooth, cold wind.

At first she thought the pony had gone into that strange fifth gait that only Icelandic ponies do. But the animals were leaping up and falling back. They couldn't reach the horse. Katie was puzzled. Then she realized what was happening. The pony was flying! The little Icelandic pony, with Katie clinging to her mane, rose slowly into the sky, the pursuers getting smaller, yapping and leaping and falling back in confusion.

It was just like her Pegasus dream, though this time there were no wings. This was different, but the same. Pegasus, the flying horse. Her pony, the flying horse.

The air was cold and clear and the stars hung above her in the northern sky, so near she felt she could reach out and touch them. The wind rushed by.

Her fear fell away like a discarded jacket replaced by calmness and silence. Even the rushing wind was silent. The silence surrounded and lifted the girl and the frightened little horse and comforted them.

She wanted it to last forever. The sudden peace and the brightness and beauty of the stars. But the pony was circling now and slowly descending. They landed with a little thud.

The field was empty. No yelping. No attackers. No wind. Nothing but the snow and, far away, the lights of cars on the highway.

The snow got brighter. At first the extra light puzzled her, then Katie looked at the sky. It was alive with shimmering, pulsating green light. The northern lights! She sat on a still Peggy, watching the lights dance across the sky until they began to fade. Then she realized how tired she was, and how cold. She wearily wondered if Peggy had seen the lights before in Iceland, but of course she'd never know.

The pony trotted to the barn, and stood with its head bowed in exhaustion as Katie slid the heavy door open. Then it clopped wearily across the cement floor to its stall.

Katie wet the end of a grain sack and gently wiped the dried blood from her pony's nose. She found some salve and daubed it on. The little horse stood, peering through her forelock at Katie with those patient, mysterious, dark eyes. Katie knew now what the mystery was. Her pony could fly! She added some fresh straw to its bed. Then, having done all she could to make the mare comfortable, she left.

Katie was hardly aware of the road home. The wondrous ride

was still swirling in her mind. The terror of the mad flight from the pursuers had evaporated. Her heart was full and happy, for the first time in weeks.

Siggi was in bed when she got home. Mom and Dad were reading. They looked up, smiling expectantly, their eyes wary but hopeful. She paused in front of them, opened her mouth, but no words came out. She was afraid to tell them about being chased by wild animals, in case they said it was too dangerous for her to ride alone. And how could she tell them what had happened when the pony had escaped from those pursuers? If she spoke, it might all fall away—the pictures in her mind, the feel of flight, the northern lights, the singing in her heart. She merely smiled, said good night, and went to bed.

She lay in the darkness, reliving each precious moment of the magical ride. She thought of her pony. Her very own magical pony. Her pony with no name.

Her pony could fly like Pegasus, the mythical steed. But Pegasus was the name of a powerful stallion, not a shaggy-coated, short-legged, homely little horse. She needed a name that suggested something small. Peggy! That was it!

She fell asleep and dreamed of a flickering curtain of northern lights in the sky and of riding Peggy, her beloved Peggy, high above the problems of her life.

— Chapter 8 —
A Wondrous Journey

Katie's feeling of euphoria didn't last long. It dissipated in the busyness of school and work and the humdrum of daily routine. When she rode Peggy, the mare dutifully trotted along but did not show any inclination to fly. When Katie urged her to a gallop, nothing happened other than a fast ride across the field.

Mom and Dad continued their campaign to involve her in solving Siggi's problems. The teacher called them in to discuss again his daydreaming and his lack of interest in schoolwork. When they got home after the meeting, they had a serious talk with Katie.

"Katie, it's important that you accept Siggi," said Mom. "Your dad and I are doing all we can but we need your help. Will you spend some time with him?"

"He doesn't like me any more than I like him," Katie argued. "He's mean. I don't think he'd like me hanging around him. Besides, I don't have time."

Mom and Dad looked exasperated. "Katie," said Dad, "couldn't you try for a while? It might make all the difference."

Katie didn't know what to say next. Every fibre of her being was rebelling against agreeing to spend time with The Kid. The interloper. The thief of family happiness. But she loved her parents. She wanted their love and trust and admiration. She wanted things to be normal again.

"Okay. I'll try," she agreed reluctantly. She decided to begin by helping out with Skippy. He was a cute, uncomplicated little dog who liked to lick faces and wag his tail. Siggi adored Skippy but he didn't always follow through on his promise to care for him.

The next day Siggi balked at taking Skippy for a walk. He wanted to watch TV.

"I'll take him this time," Katie said. She snapped the leash onto Skippy's collar.

"Thank you, Katie," was all Mom said, but the smile in her eyes said much more.

Siggi said a hasty "Thanks," but he didn't sound enthusiastic. He was already concentrating on his show.

Katie jogged with Skippy to Haggarty's. She left him in the barn with his leash fastened to a nail sticking out of the wall while she took Peggy for a short ride. Afterwards, she jogged home with Skippy. The little dog didn't look tired yet, so Katie decided to play his favourite game. She threw clumps of snow in the air and Skippy leaped for them, snatching at them with his teeth, barking excitedly.

When Skippy finally showed signs of tiring, panting between leaps, tongue hanging out, she took him inside. The television was shut off and Siggi was nowhere to be seen.

"I think he went to his room," said Mom. "He must be doing his homework—he's awfully quiet. Dad's gone to do the grocery shopping and I have to fix supper. Would you mind checking on him?"

Katie peeked through Siggi's open door but he wasn't there. Then she saw the door to her room was closed even though she distinctly remembered leaving it open. Mom had her back to Katie. She was chopping vegetables and adding them to the pot of soup simmering on the wood stove while she hummed softly along with the radio.

Katie turned the doorknob to her room. It resisted. She twisted harder and the door sprang open. Siggi was standing in front of her, his hand on the knob, his eyes wide and frightened. He stared for a fraction of a second, then rushed past her. Katie was too surprised to say anything.

Mom didn't notice where Siggi had come from. "Have you finished your homework?" she asked him.

"The teacher said to read a book," he responded. "Can Dad listen to me read it later, Mrs. McKay?"

"I'm sure he'd like to do that." Mom's voice was low and cheerful. She was happy that Siggi said Dad, even though he still called her Mrs. McKay.

Katie felt her fingernails biting into her palms. He's my dad, not yours.

She scanned her room. Nothing seemed out of place. Her clothes were still hanging on a row of hooks along the end wall. Her stuffed animals were lined up on her dresser, as usual. Then she noticed something dark poking out from under the bedspread where it touched the floor at the foot of her bed.

It was the box in which she kept her Victorian dolls and their clothes. She jerked the lid off and dumped the contents on the bed. She pawed through everything.

"Mom! Come and see what he's done now!" she screamed. Search as she might, she couldn't find Samantha.

By the time Dad returned, Katie had quieted down. She had stopped shouting and was nursing a quiet, cold fury.

"I didn't touch your stupid dolls," Siggi insisted for the fifth time.

"I'm at my wits' end," Mom said. "Magnetic dolls don't just vanish into thin air. Perhaps you misplaced it, Katie."

Siggi looked Dad in the eye. "I only went into Katie's room to look out the window to see what Skippy was doing," he said evenly. "I heard him barking behind the cabin."

He's an out-and-out liar, Katie thought, and still Mom and Dad accept everything he says. She was fuming. It seemed she couldn't change their attitude to him so she'd just give up trying. She glowered.

An hour later, after Katie grudgingly helped her parents prepare supper, they were all seated at the table, eating thick beef and vegetable soup. Mom, Dad, and Siggi were chatting between mouthfuls. How can they act as if nothing has happened? thought Katie. They must know he did it. He deliberately went into my stuff and took my favourite thing, and they don't care one little bit. As long as their precious little Siggi is happy, they don't care at all if I'm alive or dead. I'll show them!

Ravenously hungry, Katie dug into her soup, trying to think how to show her parents how deeply hurt and angry she was. She was lost in thought when she realized that the conversation around her had stopped. Someone must have asked her something, for when she looked up, all eyes were on her. They were clearly waiting for an answer.

"What?" she asked, searching their expectant faces.

"You played with my dog, so I should be 'lowed to ride your horse," said Siggi.

"How about it, Katie?" asked Dad. "Seems like a fair exchange to me."

She sat there a moment, stunned. They couldn't mean it. They knew how she felt about anyone else riding Peggy.

"Katie," Mom said, then bit her lower lip. Her voice was low and intense. "You did play with Skippy for nearly an hour today and Siggi didn't say a word. I don't think a ten-minute ride on your pony is too much for him to ask in return. Siggi says he didn't touch your doll and I believe him. Your attitude is inexcusable."

Katie gasped. Her pain was almost unbearable.

"Katie," Dad was frowning, "after supper, I want you to go back to Haggarty's, help Siggi onto your horse, and lead it around the corral. Ten minutes sounds adequate. Now I don't want to hear another word."

Katie dropped her spoon onto the floor. It hit with a clatter in the expectant silence as they waited for her response. She got unsteadily to her feet and stumbled to the door where she pulled on her outdoor pants, parka, and boots. She opened the door and a cold draft surged in. She turned and looked at the three of them staring at her.

"Peggy is mine," she said, her voice shaking. "I only played with Skippy because Siggi didn't want to. I thought I was helping out. And all I get is a bawling out and... and..." Tears were choking her. She saw Mom half-rising from her chair, but she didn't wait to hear what she was going to say. Katie ran outside, slamming the door behind her. She ran and ran, tears freezing on her cheeks. She reached Haggarty's barn, panting from her long run, and rolled the door open just far enough to squeeze inside.

Peggy looked over the wall of her stall and nickered a greeting. Katie ran to her and threw her arms around the pony's thick neck. She buried her face in the coarse mane, and sobbed. Peggy stood quietly, once or twice turning her calm face to look at the heart-broken girl.

Katie parted the forelock and looked into the horse's eyes through a blur of tears. Her sobs faded to a few hiccups. She rubbed the tears away with her mitten so she could see clearly. The big, black, liquid eyes looking into hers were full of compassion. The mare nickered softly again, and rubbed her velvet nose, healed smoothly now, on Katie's arm.

"Oh, Peggy," Katie sighed. "You're the only one who understands. You and Samantha," she amended. She felt a little disloyal, for Peggy was becoming more important to her than Samantha. Then she remembered that her doll was gone and she felt sobs rising in her throat once again. She laid her face against the pony's neck and breathed deeply, inhaling the warm, slightly dusty smell of the animal's coat.

When she thought of the missing Samantha doll, the peace she felt in the dim quiet barn began to evaporate. How could he! Why would he be so cruel?

As her rage returned, she knew she had to do something or explode. She grabbed the bridle from the wall beside the stall. Peggy obediently opened her mouth so Katie could slip in the bit.

In minutes she was riding her pony behind the barn. There was some visibility, but she knew how reckless she was when she urged the pony to a gallop. Dad and Mom would be shocked by her lack of responsibility. She knew the pony could trip in the dim light and throw her. Why, she might be killed. That would show them, she thought. She envisioned them finding her broken body in the snow. She saw them crying and saying that they really loved her after all. When she thought of them crying, she cried harder than before, wetting the scarf across her face.

The pony bounded forward. When she felt the difference, she recognized what was happening and her body filled with excitement. The jolting gallop faded away and she was riding smoothly, effortlessly, soaring above the earth. This time there were no wild animals, just Katie's wild and angry thoughts chasing her. And the mare had responded to Katie's desperation by carrying her away from her anger, high above the bleakness of her life, high among the peace and beauty of the stars.

All too soon, Peggy swung to the right. The last time Peggy had flown, she had circled before she landed. Katie didn't want to go back, back to where she had left her angry thoughts, so she pulled hard on the left rein and the pony responded. She flew straight on and on.

The next time the pony began circling, Katie didn't try to stop her. Her stomach growled. She hadn't finished supper. She was hungry.

As Peggy descended in her lazy, circuitous way, they were enveloped in a cloud. Katie could see nothing. This didn't surprise her. This time, her flight among the stars had felt wonderful, but normal.

Peggy was hovering now. Katie looked down, listening for yelps. There was no sound but the wind. Light shimmered through the cloudy air, but still she could see nothing. Peggy's hooves touched earth, and Katie felt a little shudder ripple through her. The mare was trotting again, her hooves clicking against a hard surface, not muffled as they would have been in the snow. Katie didn't understand. She was puzzled and just a little frightened.

She let the reins hang loose. Peggy trotted confidently along as if she knew exactly where she was. Since they were no longer flying, Katie figured they were not in a cloud but were enveloped by fog. Lights shone at intervals, making shining spheres in the mist but for long bewildering moments she could see nothing clearly. However, she could hear. And smell.

Peggy shied to the left and a dark hazy shape rattled by on the right-hand side. The sound was of wheels clattering over stones. The fog was polluted with smoke and something else, sharp and stinging to her eyes and throat. It was like manure, but more rank. Something really strange was going on.

The fog thinned in the glow of a street light. The light was high on an iron post and it flickered like a flame. Katie couldn't believe what she was seeing! Peggy was trotting on a street with teams of bigger horses pulling high-wheeled vehicles past them.

A woman stepped into the glow of a street light and stood there, waiting for them to pass before she crossed the street. Katie could see the woman's silhouette through the haze. She was wearing a hat and a long garment that she pulled up from her boot tops before she stepped from the curb into the muddy street. It's all so weird, like a dream, Katie thought.

Peggy abruptly made a left turn. They were on some kind of narrow path, with no street lights. The mare suddenly stopped and refused to move even when Katie urged her forward. It was as if she had reached the end of a journey. Katie slipped from her pony's back. It was too dark to see, so she put out her hand and touched something hard and rough, a wall of some kind.

She was thinking that they should go back to the busy street, when she heard a scraping sound, like rusty hinges. A door opened in the wall and someone approached, carrying a lantern. The person stopped in front of them and raised the lantern high. Its pale beams shone around Katie and her shaggy pony. Katie stared back at a girl holding the lantern. She had a shawl over her head and was clutching it under her chin.

"You've come!" the girl said in a voice full of emotion. "Ah, I knew you'd come if I wished hard enough!"

Katie stepped close to Peggy and put her hand on the pony's neck for support. She felt a little dizzy. It was one thing to have a horse that could fly, but now the world had truly turned upside down. For standing in front of her was a living breathing human being. Samantha!

Chapter 9

A Visitor From A Far Country

"I've been waiting for you," said Samantha. "I've wanted you to come for ever so long. Come with me."

Katie wordlessly followed, leading Peggy. She decided it might be best to just see what would happen next. As she passed through the gate, Katie felt something in the way of her legs every time she took a step. She looked down and saw, with a shock, that she was wearing an ankle-length skirt like one in her book on Victorian England. Showing beneath the hem were sturdy laced boots with a narrow toe, and above these a bit of knitted stocking showed. Her hand went to her throat. The locket was still there, but that seemed to be the only thing she had from home. She stroked the cool silver for comfort. Peggy nickered. Her locket wasn't the only familiar thing here in this strange world.

Katie followed Samantha to a shed at the back of the yard, behind a tall narrow brick house. Samantha was chattering all the way. How had the trip been? Had coming into the past frightened her? Katie didn't answer. Her mind was whirling. She was busy trying to take everything in. Besides, Samantha didn't seem to expect replies.

Inside the shed, Samantha tied Peggy's halter to a manger beside a black horse looming large and dark in the gloom, quietly munching his oats. Katie recognized him as Jimbo, the horse Samantha was riding when they met in the field.

Samantha was rattling away, still asking questions. "Do you

think Peggy finds London strange?" Katie wasn't surprised that Samantha knew Peggy's name. She seemed to know everything about these impossible happenings.

After giving Peggy some oats and a pail of water, Samantha said, "Follow me to the house. Don't be surprised if it's bigger than yours." She stopped and hugged Katie, saying, "I'm so glad you're here!" On their way across the yard Samantha chatted as though she and Katie were old friends.

"I've wanted my very own friend for the longest time," Samantha said. "I've been lonely, so I was ecstatically happy to see you in the field that day."

She led Katie to the back of the house where they descended a few steps to a door in the basement and went in. A slight young woman with shining black eyes and quick bird-like movements greeted Samantha and looked curiously at Katie. She had on a long grey dress with an apron over it and a small white cap pinned to her hair. She was carrying a coal scuttle and a brush. Katie looked around. The room must be a kitchen though she'd never seen a kitchen in a basement before. There was a long table in the middle of the room, and a four-door cupboard standing up against a wall. On another wall was a huge stove with two ovens and metal trim polished to a bright shine. She could see flames in the cracks around a little door on its front.

"Ge' way from cooker," Daisy scolded Samantha. "Mind when you burned your 'and?"

"This is Daisy," Samantha said, moving away from the hot stove. "Daisy, we have a visitor from Canada, so tell Cook there'll be another for meals."

Daisy dropped a curtsey to Samantha, but she was still looking at Katie. "Yes, Miss, I'll tell 'er. Soon's I finish warshing dishes."

Samantha nodded as if the conversation was over. Daisy set the coal scuttle down by the cooker and went through a doorway to an adjoining room. The door was open so Katie peeked in. The room had a long work table with chopping boards and sharp knives on it. Daisy took plates dripping with hot soapy water from a huge white sink and placed them in a rack on the wall. Katie could see that the little maid's hands looked red and sore.

It's like a second kitchen, thought Katie. As if she could read her thoughts, Samantha explained, "It's not a kitchen, it's just the scullery where the rough work is done," and she shut the door with energy, ending the conversation.

"Daisy didn't seem surprised to hear I was from Canada," said Katie aloud. She had finally found her tongue.

"I don't suppose Daisy knows anything about Canada," said Samantha. "She's a housemaid—didn't go to school very long. Maybe she thinks it's like being from France—somewhere close. Come with me and I'll introduce you to my parents."

"Wait a minute!" said Katie in alarm. "Maybe Daisy isn't surprised at seeing me, but your parents might know where Canada is. How are you going to explain it to them?"

"We have to keep the magic a secret. Promise me you won't tell them. They can't find out the truth. They wouldn't be able to believe it anyway. They'd likely think you were trying to take advantage of us somehow and would forbid us to be friends after all," Samantha said urgently.

"How will you explain me being here?" asked Katie.

"Oh, I'll figure that out as I go along. Come. My parents are in the morning room." Samantha led the way upstairs to the ground floor.

In a hallway at the top of the stairs, flaring gas-flamed lamps on the walls made the scroll-patterns on the red and gold wallpaper seem to undulate. Samantha paused before a door and smoothed her shoulder-length hair—brown flecked with gold—making sure it hadn't escaped from the velvet ribbon tying it back.

When Samantha opened the door Katie gasped. There, in the soft gaslight and the flickering of coal burning in a small fireplace, was a familiar scene. A bearded man in a dark suit was sitting in a wing chair near the fire. He was reading aloud from a large red book, and a boy of six or seven was stretched out on the rug at his feet, listening. A small child with curly hair was also on the floor, playing with spools on a string. The room was comfortably cluttered with books and interesting objects Katie had learned about in her reading about the Victorian era. On a table covered with a heavy fringed cloth were a stereoscope and a kaleidoscope. The walls were covered with paintings, some in rows below other rows. The mantle was covered with dried flower arrangements and shells glued to black velvet in elaborate designs. Books were piled on the floor.

Samantha went to stand next to a woman in a long blue dress that was partially covered by a grey smock. Katie recognized her immediately as the mother in her book. The woman was seated by an easel, painting the grouping by the fire. She looked up at Samantha and smiled.

"Samantha dear, like a dutiful daughter you've come just when I needed you. I want you to stand behind your father and lean on his chair just as you did last evening. I can't seem to get the curve of your shoulder..." She saw Katie and broke off.

"Mama, this is a new friend, Katie. She came to London from Canada. Now she is lost and has no one to help her. Can she stay with us for a few days? Please?"

"Lost?" said the mother. "Where are your parents, child?"

Katie looked down at the floor. She was twisting a bit of her skirt, unsure how to respond. She felt she had no choice but to answer truthfully. "They're still back in Canada." When she looked up she saw that the father had stopped reading and was staring at her with great interest, while the mother still wore an inquisitive expression. "They're so far away, they don't know I'm lost," Katie added.

"They sent her on a ship to London to visit her relatives and when she got here after weeks and weeks her relatives were all gone. So she has no one. She was in the park, riding on a pony, completely lost when I met her. I put the pony in the shed with Jimbo. I hope I did the right thing," Samantha reamed off breathlessly. It was obvious she felt no shame at creating a story to explain Katie's sudden appearance.

"Rode on a pony?" asked the astonished mother.

"From the East End. Where her relatives live," Samantha repeated.

"The East End," repeated the mother. Then Katie saw the woman exchange a look with her husband that seemed to say, No wonder she can't find her relatives in a place like that.

What's the matter with the East End? wondered Katie. She was starting to relax a little. Samantha seemed able to produce answers for any difficult questions and cover for Katie's ignorance.

"She hasn't eaten since she got to London, Mother," said Samantha with a deliberate look of concern.

The mother awoke from the spell cast by Samantha's far-fetched story. Without rising from her chair, she seemed to bustle into action.

"Hungry, my dear?" She didn't wait for an answer. "Samantha, take her to the kitchen and ask Daisy to make her some bread and milk. Then, take her to your room. She can sleep on the cot until we find her relatives." She turned to her husband. "Perhaps we could put a notice in the Times, John. Enquiring as to their whereabouts."

"I doubt if they read the Times in the East End, my dear," answered the father, smiling fondly, just as he did in Katie's book.

Katie followed Samantha downstairs to the kitchen. At Samantha's request, Daisy cut a slice off a loaf she got from under a white cloth, broke the bread into pieces, put the pieces in a bowl, covered them with milk, then sprinkled sugar over it all. Katie was so hungry that she began eating immediately. She was surprised at how good it tasted.

Katie's mind was whirling with a thousand questions. For now she asked, "Are your parents always this easy to convince?"

Samantha just laughed.

"What will happen when they find out you made up the whole story?"

"Don't worry. They won't find out," Samantha answered in a soothing voice. "I did make one mistake. I said your relatives live in the East End. I would have impressed them if I'd picked somewhere more fashionable. Still, the East End is a big place so they can't possibly search every house. Besides, they always believe what I tell them."

Samantha looked so sure of herself. Katie felt a mixture of admiration for her friend's self-assurance, and disappointment that she was so disrespectful of her parents. After all, they're just like they are in my book, she thought. Absolutely perfect.

Feeling much better now that she'd eaten, Katie followed Samantha up the stairs from the basement kitchen to the hallway with its red and gold wallpaper, up a grander set of stairs with a smooth shiny banister, up yet another stairway to the third floor, then through a doorway and up another narrower set of stairs with no banister at all, into a large room with a rocking horse in front of yet another fireplace. Toys were scattered about. "This is the nursery," Samantha announced.

The girls went from the nursery directly into Samantha's bedroom. In it was a four-poster bed, a dresser with a matching washstand, a trunk, a rocking chair, and, in the corner, a cot.

Samantha gestured toward the cot. "This is where you will sleep. It was put here for Nanny so she could be nearby when I was sick."

Samantha rummaged in a trunk, brought out an elaborate white nightgown, and tossed it to Katie. "This is too small for me now," she said. "It should fit you."

Katie did as Samantha did. She removed her dress and stockings. When Samantha removed her corsets, Katie followed suit, although instead of corsets she was wearing a vest over an undershirt. Then both girls pulled their nightgowns over their heads and over their underwear, then snuggled into their beds.

No sooner were they covered up than the door opened and a stern-looking woman came in to turn out the lights. "Nanny, this is Katie," said Samantha sleepily.

"I've spoken to Madam so I know your friend will be staying with us until she can be returned safely to her family," Nanny said. She tucked them in. When she left, Katie said, "Your family must be very rich to have so many servants."

"Nonsense," said Samantha. "We have only Cook, Daisy, and Billy who does the heavy work and looks after Jimbo and the gig. Nanny's not really a servant. She's a gentlewoman—poor and in need of a salary—but a gentlewoman nonetheless. Rich people have ever so many more servants with butlers and grooms and everything. Father has an important position in the city, in a bank. He says we're not rich, but we're respectable."

Katie heard this but she didn't answer. She didn't know what a gig was but she was too tired to ask.

— Chapter 10 —
The East End

Katie woke with a start, but when she remembered where she was she stretched lazily and happily. She reviewed the happenings of the previous day. Peggy, her little pony that she was coming to love so much, could fly not only through space, but through time! She marvelled at the very idea. And she had been brought back in time to the very family she'd been admiring in her Victorian book. Ever since she'd seen Samantha in the field, she'd been hoping she was real, and here she was, a living, breathing girl. Katie pinched herself to make sure she wasn't dreaming, and smiled when the pinch hurt. The pain meant that this was no dream! She wondered how she would get home again, but decided she didn't have to worry about that yet.

For now, she could luxuriate in the fact that a girl her own age, and a girl as sure of herself and her place in the world as Samantha was, wanted to be friends with her. The slight disappointment she had felt in Samantha yesterday had disappeared in the pleasure of having a new friend. She was also pleased that she was living in this lovely house with Samantha and her perfect family, just as she had longed to do.

Samantha groaned and got out of bed. "Hurry and get dressed, Katie," she ordered. "We have to eat early for Papa to get to his office by seven o'clock." She saw Katie looking around in wonderment and added, "I guess you'll have to get used to a few things here. For one thing, we don't have a flush toilet in our house yet, although all the rich people have them. Papa says we'll get one soon," she said brightly. "They're ever so modern. I'm sure everyone has one where you come from."

"Many people have several. But we don't have one in our cabin," said Katie. Samantha's room had a wash bowl and pitcher on the washstand, and a chamber pot of matching china decorated with pink flowers peeking out from under the bed. Grandma likes antiques so much, she would love to have such a pretty set, Katie thought as she poured warm water from the pitcher into the wash bowl.

The dining room was on the second floor, above the morning room. It was darker, more claustrophobic. The top part of the walls was painted dark green, the bottom was panelled with dark wood. The drapes were of heavy velvet and half-covered the windows, keeping out much of the daylight. The table and sideboard were also made of dark wood. "The furniture is mahogany, which is ever so exotic," Samantha said. The table was covered with gleaming silver dishes and cutlery and had many twinkling glasses at each place. The room felt cluttered just as the morning room had, but with fancier, more expensive clutter.

Cook must have been up in the wee hours to prepare the huge breakfast. Daisy brought in covered silver dishes and put them on the sideboard, some over candles to keep them warm. Katie followed Samantha, plate in hand. The girls helped themselves to scrambled eggs, lamb's kidneys, salty fish, fried potatoes, stewed tomatoes, and baked beans. On the table were silver racks of freshly buttered toast and a sparkly glass jar of marmalade in a silver holder that hung on a little swing from a silver frame. Katie was very hungry and dug in with such enthusiasm that Samantha sat back and laughed at her.

"Where are your little brothers?" asked Katie, wondering why the boys weren't at breakfast.

"In the nursery, of course. Nanny's feeding them there."

Samantha's parents didn't say anything about finding Katie's relatives. In fact they barely acknowledged her and seemed to have forgotten everything that was said last evening. Strange, thought Katie. After they finished their second cups of tea, Samantha's father put on his waistcoat, his black overcoat, and grey top hat with matching grey gloves, then took his walking stick, kissed his wife on the cheek, and left for the station. "He takes an underground train to his office in the city," explained Samantha. Katie thought he looked both handsome and important.

After he left, Samantha's mother said, "I'm going to my dress-maker now, to pick up an afternoon gown."

"Oh, good," said Samantha. "Your other gowns are terribly out of style."

"Yes, I simply had to have one made in the new fashion, without a bustle," agreed the mother. Putting on her new flat hat, she said, "While I'm gone, you may ride in the park, but you must be back, changed, and in the nursery by the time Nanny puts Elbert down for his morning nap. Nanny will give you girls your French lesson then, while Wilbur plays in the nursery."

Back in Samantha's room, the girls found that Daisy had already laid out their riding costumes. Normally Katie looked after her own clothes, but it didn't seem that Samantha did anything for herself. Sure enough, when they left the house by the kitchen door, they were met by Billy, who had their horses saddled and waiting for them.

Samantha rode on Jimbo, his fat black rump swaying behind her slim body. She was dressed in proper riding habit, seated on a proper side-saddle, her gold-flecked hair tumbling onto her shoulders from beneath her perky hat, her riding crop clutched in one properly gloved hand. In Katie's eyes she was absolutely beautiful.

Behind her, little Peggy had to trot to keep up to Jimbo with his much longer legs. On her back, very likely for the first time in her life, was a sidesaddle, and on that saddle sat Katie, dressed much the same as Samantha, one leg over a kind of post that kept her from slipping off. Both leg and post were well hidden by her long skirt. Riding like this felt strange, but Katie thought she must look elegant so she persevered. She was especially happy to be riding again on her sweet little Peggy, the only other constant, besides the locket, in her turned-upside-down world.

The girls were riding in a park, near Samantha's home. There were other horses and ponies as well as numerous bicycles on narrow roads through the park, their riders "taking their exercise" as Samantha put it. "Some of the equestrians here are from our neighbourhood," Samantha explained. "Others come from farther away and are very rich, indeed. Especially those riding elegant horses." While the bicycles were different from what she was used to, Katie thought they looked surprisingly modern, the main exception being that the female cyclists wore long skirts.

Back at Samantha's, Katie should have found the French lesson easy, for she was in a French immersion class at home. But Nanny had the strangest accent, making her French difficult to under-stand, and most of the lesson consisted of rapid-fire verb conjuga-tions. Katie did as well as she could, but she wasn't familiar with some of the conjugations, so she made many mistakes. However, as poorly as she did, Samantha did worse.

Samantha was clearly uninterested. She yawned and gawked

out the window and got lost in her tenses. Once, Nanny got so
cross that she picked up a ruler and whacked it across Samantha's
knuckles. Katie was shocked. This would never happen in her
school. Samantha glowered and rubbed her red knuckles, but she
didn't seem too upset and Katie noticed that she began paying attention to the lesson—for a while.

After lunch in the nursery, the girls had two free hours while
Nanny took the two little boys for a walk in the park. The girls
waved good-bye to Nanny going down the path with baby Elbert
in the pram and seven-year-old Wilbur trotting at her side.
Samantha asked Katie if she had any little brothers.

"Just Siggi," said Katie. "And he's not really my brother. In fact,
I don't like him much. Don't you remember? I told the Samantha
doll all about this."

"Yes, of course I remember," said Samantha. "I also remember
how upset you were when he came to your family."

"And I remember how good it felt to tell my troubles to someone, even though I didn't know you were real. I wished you were,
though."

"Touch me. I'm real all right! Now," she continued, "Daisy is
supposed to be watching us, but Cook has her in the kitchen doing chores, so she won't notice we're missing. We have time to go
to the East End. I have a friend there I want you to meet. I met
him in the park months ago and I think he's the nicest boy I've
ever met, but my parents won't hear of us being friends because
he doesn't live in the right part of London. You see, Katie, you're
not the only one who has problems with parents."

Your problems aren't anything like mine, Katie thought. But
she didn't interrupt. Samantha went on. "My big mistake was to
introduce Nicholas to Mama and Papa. I should have kept our

friendship a secret. A few days later Mama saw him at the park gate with another boy selling things from a barrow. She told Papa and they said I wasn't to see him again. Since then, I've been to visit him in his home many times. My parents don't know and they'll never find out unless you tell them!" Samantha gave Katie a warning look. "Don't say a word about where we're going or we'll never be allowed on our own again!"

Katie didn't reply, but Samantha's willingness to defy her parents made her feel somewhat uneasy.

For the second time that day, they put on their riding clothes. Before they left, Samantha poked her head in the kitchen to see what the servants were doing. Daisy had her head in a cloud of steam as she poured broth into a black cauldron on the huge iron cooker. She waved a wooden spoon toward them as if to tell them to just go and stop bothering her.

The horses were rested and fed, so they trotted smartly along the muddy streets, avoiding the deep ruts made by carriages and gigs, which Katie now knew was a light two-wheeled carriage. Winter hadn't started here yet, but it was damp and she felt the cold. She shivered.

The girls passed from the pleasant area where Samantha and her family lived. With no fog blocking her view today, Katie could see rows and rows of identical houses, each joined to a twin, with identical little stairways behind metal railings from the street down to the basements where the kitchens were, and identical little stairways up from the street to the front doors. Each house had many chimneys belching coal smoke into the leaden skies.

The street ran past the big park, with its many trees and paths and gates and ponds, where Nanny had taken the boys. They rode by the park to avoid being spotted by Nanny and travelled a long distance until they came to an entirely different neighbourhood. No trees here. And there were more people in the streets, all shouting and singing and selling things from carts.

"Buy my fat chickens!" someone yelled in a singsong voice.

"Fair cherries, sixpence a pound!" sang another.

"Hawkers," said Samantha.

There weren't so many fancy carriages here, and the roads were, if anything, dirtier and more hazardous.

Two men came down the street. As they passed, Katie heard one say, "'Is nime's 'arry." Samantha laughed at the puzzled look on her face. "They have a working class accent and they don't pronounce h's," she explained. "He said, 'His name's Harry.'

"Welcome to the East End," she laughed, "where I'm not supposed to go. And for that matter, Katie, you shouldn't either." Katie wondered why not, but returned her friend's grin, and decided to find out for herself.

Chapter II

Mother James

"This is where we'll stop," said Samantha. "We can tie our horses over there." She led Katie to a post that had iron rings where they tied their horses, then up the street and around the corner to a busy main street that Samantha called the high street. Samantha stopped in front of a shop. Above the door hung a sign: Nicholas Camper, Master Bootmaker.

The brick building had unpainted splintery mouldings around the doors. Beside a large window with a neat display of boots was a door that led into the shop, but Samantha pointed to another door beside it. "My friend, Nicholas, lives upstairs."

"Your friend is the bootmaker?" Katie asked, puzzled.

"My friend is the bootmaker's son. They have the same name."

As they approached the doorway, a gang of boys entered the street from an alley and blocked their way. Katie felt a chill of apprehension, and stepped closer to Samantha. There were seven or eight boys, some quite small, but two or three were older and taller, including the one in front, who seemed to be the leader. They slowly moved closer to the girls, staring at them menacingly. They all wore dirty, ragged clothes. All had rags wrapped around their feet, except the leader who wore a pair of fine leather boots and had a cloth cap pulled down over his eyes, the brim bent upward in the centre like a little tunnel so he could see. He had dark, beady eyes that glittered in the shade of his cap. He stared at the girls, scanned the street, then stared at them again.

"'Ello mites! Wot 'ave we 'ere," he said to the other boys. His voice was raspy and mocking.

"A couple o' fine lidies. Look at 'em fancies! Wot're lidies like you doin' down 'ere, moight I awsk?" he said sarcastically.

The little boys in the gang looked to the speaker with a mixture of fear and admiration; the others kept staring at the girls. Katie clutched Samantha's hand.

Samantha glared at the gang. "Let us by," she said imperiously.

"Let us by!" repeated the boy with the cap in a high, mocking voice. "Let us by or us'll ...," his voice dropped a notch, "or us'll do wot?"

"We've come to visit a friend, and his father will see you, so let us by!" Samantha ordered.

The boy with the cap began to laugh. He glanced at his gang, pointed to the sign above the shop door, and laughed harder. The other boys took a minute as if they weren't sure they had permission, then they began to laugh with him.

"If 'e sees us it'll be roit strange since 'e's dead an' planted." He raised his hand and the laughter stopped. He had just spotted the chain around Katie's neck. The gang all paused, followed his gaze, and stared at the locket. Katie's hand went up to her throat and covered it. No one could take this away from her. It held the picture of her and her parents—her family.

Without warning, like a coiled snake that suddenly strikes, the boy with the cap sprang toward them. The girls, already frightened and tense, turned and raced back toward the horses.

They ran with a fleetness born of fear. Running feet thudded behind them as they turned the corner. The horses were in sight. Jimbo was dozing on his feet, but Peggy jerked her head up, startled by the ruckus. There was no way, Katie realized with a sick feeling, that they could slow down enough to mount the horses without being caught. She could hear the ragged breaths of the boys getting closer. She expected a hand to reach out and grab her collar or snatch the locket from around her neck.

The leader cried out, and the sound of running feet stopped in a cacophony of shouts and curses. Katie and Samantha ran a little farther before they dared to look back. The leader had fallen and several of his gang had tripped over him and over each other; they were tangled in a heap. While the boys were getting up, Samantha grabbed Katie by the wrist, and pulled her into a side street. They ran for their lives. Seeing an open doorway, they bounded up the sagging steps and slipped through.

The boys came thundering around the corner as the girls ducked out of sight. Katie covered her nose; they were in a dim hallway that smelled like vomit. Samantha buried her nose in Katie's shoulder. Their hearts pounding, the girls cowered in the corner of the hallway near the door, trying to slow their breath, hoping the boys hadn't seen them.

"'Ere ya be!" The boy with the cap reached in, grabbed Katie by her hair, and pulled. Samantha screamed, grasped Katie's riding jacket to keep her from being pulled outside, and with her free hand whacked the boy on the arm. But the boy was too strong for them. He didn't let go. With the other hand he was clawing at Katie's throat for the locket, while she tried to beat his arm back. The doorway darkened as the other boys crowded in after him.

"Ay up ragamuffins! Let 'em go!" a cracked voice shouted from behind them. "Let 'em go or I'll give you little boogers a whop yer not likely t' fergit!"

With a last pull at her hair, making Katie scream with pain, the leader let go, then ran into the street. The gang ran after him, disappearing around the corner.

"There now girlies," said the gravelly voice. "That's done and got rid o' that Pod. 'E's a bad un."

Rubbing her stinging scalp, Katie turned to see a man waving a dirty rag mop. No, she was mistaken, for although the figure was tall, had muscular arms and huge feet in cracked leather boots, it was definitely a woman. She was wearing a dress hanging to her ankles, so dirty that Katie couldn't guess the colour, and her hair was pulled to the top of her head in a knob. Her nose was large and red.

"Come in, dearies, and ketch yer breath."

Still shaking, the girls followed the giant into a room nearby. Embers glowed in a small fireplace, giving a little light to see by, but not giving enough heat to drive away the damp chill. The one window was so grimy and covered with crawling flies that it was nearly impervious to light. Then Katie noticed a sort of rustling and scraping sound. She thought it might be animals; the suspicion of rats made her move back toward the doorway, but she bumped into Samantha and stopped.

Her eyes were starting to adjust to the dim light and she saw what was making the noise. Children filled the room. Two sat on the floor in front of the hearth, while four more were on chairs at a wooden table. A baby gave a kitten-like cry from a box in the corner.

"Come in, come in," said the woman, even though both girls were already in and Katie was wishing they weren't. The room had the sour, sickish smell they'd first encountered in the hall, but it was stronger here. Even Samantha, who had seemed brave enough a few minutes ago, was now eyeing the doorway nervously.

"Those lads are bad uns, an' that Pod's the wors' of the bunch. 'E's been thievin' and fightin' since 'e was in nappies. 'E likes t' be cruel. You'd bes' stop 'ere a little 'til they're far off." She seemed to notice for the first time their riding clothes and leather boots. Suddenly her mood changed. A look of anger crossed her face. "You've no right bein' down 'ere where yuz don' belong," she growled.

She reached for a bottle on the shelf above the fire, uncorked it, took a deep swig of its colourless contents, then re-corked it, slapped the cork for good measure, and returned it to its shelf.

The woman shuddered. In a moment her demeanour changed and she said in a friendly voice, "Me nime's Mother Jimes, and wot might your nimes be?" Without waiting for the answer, she plunged her mop into a pail of dirty water, wrung it out, and made some swipes at the filthy floor.

"I'm Katie and this is Samantha," Katie said, trying not to look disgusted. She had been taught to be polite.

The baby started wailing seriously, like a weak cat, and a waif of a girl, maybe five or six years old, picked it up. The baby was wrapped in a scrap of blanket and its face was pale and wizened like the faces of the other children.

Katie wanted desperately to leave.

Mother James shouted at the children on two of the chairs, "Get yourselves off so girlies can set and ketch breath." While the girls sat, stiff and awkward, they stared at the children who, except the girl holding the baby, were all busy making brushes of some kind. Thin and sickly, they worked steadily. Now and then, between putting a finished brush in a box on the floor and getting more materials from the table for the next one, one of them would look at the visitors with big wondering eyes. Katie and Samantha must have looked like royalty, wearing such fine clothes. Katie touched her lapels self-consciously.

Abruptly, Mother James's mood changed again. She roared at a child when it dropped a brush, then she turned to the girls angrily. "Wot er ya sittin' 'round 'ere fer? The little uns are all lookin' at yez and fergettin' t' work."

She lunged at them. "Sling yer 'ook! Get outta m'sight, or I'll give y' somethin' y' won't fergit!"

For the second time that afternoon, Katie and Samantha were on their feet and running. No one was chasing them, but they didn't stop until they were near the post where they'd tethered the horses.

Katie noticed it first, and skidded to a stop. Samantha ran on a few steps, then she stopped, too. Jimbo was jerking his head against the rope that tied him to the post. He stood alone. Peggy was gone.

— Chapter 12 —
Nicholas

"Those boys!" Samantha said angrily.

Katie was frantic. She scanned the street. If Peggy's rope had come untied, she'd be nearby. But no. No pony. Samantha was likely right. The pony had been stolen. Her blood was boiling. Katie looked for a policeman, but there was no sign of one. And no sign of boys leading away a shaggy pony. Her beloved pony, her only way of getting home, was nowhere to be seen.

"Let's go up to Nicholas's place," said Samantha. "He'll know what we should do."

Katie followed. She didn't know what else to do. She shrank back at the door to the flat fearing another dank apartment and another nasty Mother James. But the woman who answered the door was nothing like Mother James.

She was petite and neatly dressed. She smiled when she saw Samantha. "Oh, it's m' boy's frien'. An' she's brought someone wif 'er. Yer mos' welcome t' me 'ome. Come in, come in."

The room was small, but it was scrupulously clean. It was furnished with a sideboard, a round dining table with four chairs, a rug on the rough boards of the floor, and a couple of well-worn but comfortable-looking chairs. The window was covered with lace curtains. On the windowsill was a bright red geranium and under it was a small table holding a sewing basket. Spilling from the over-filled basket was a little cushion bristling with pins, spools of thread with loose ends touching the floor, and a measuring tape that trailed its unwound tail onto the table. Beside the table was a small rocking chair padded with cushions. A tiny coal-burning stove in a fireplace made the room cozy. After the gloomy, sour-smelling room that Mother James and her brood lived in, Katie was relieved to find herself in a place which, while not as large and elegant as Samantha's home, was fly-free, clean, decent, and warm.

"Mrs. Camper, Nicholas, I want you to meet my friend, Katie, who has come all the way from Canada," Samantha said to the woman whose smile was warm, and to the boy who looked down during the introductions.

So this was Samantha's friend, Nicholas. When he raised his head, she looked into round blue eyes. He looked vaguely familiar but she couldn't imagine why. He impressed her as being intelligent, and kind. She could see why Samantha wanted him for a friend. Even though she had just met him, she already felt friendly toward him.

"I heard Mr. Camper passed away," Samantha said politely. "Is this true?"

"Killed," said Nicholas. "By team runaway 'orses. In fronta shop." His eyes flashed with anger. Mrs. Camper dabbed at fresh tears rolling down her cheeks. Nicholas took his mother's arm and led her to a chair.

"I'm so sorry," said Samantha.

After a moment of silence during which Mrs. Camper struggled to control her emotions, Nicholas remembered his manners. "Please, sit," he said to the girls.

In their sadness, Nicholas and his mother reminded Katie of Siggi and of how much he missed his mother. She thought of her own parents. She could only imagine how she would feel if one of them died. She felt truly sorry for these people. Then she remembered why she and Samantha had come.

"Nicholas, can you tell us what to do to get my little horse back?" she blurted. "She was stolen from where we left her, not far from here."

An expression crossed Nicholas's face so quickly, Katie wasn't sure if he was frightened, angry, or both. She was puzzled until she realized that, since his father's death, Nicholas must think all horses were dangerous and frightening.

"Sorry, I was on m' way out," said Mrs. Camper. "But m' boy can 'elp ya wif yer 'orse. Long's 'e stays put. An' 'e can get y' lassies cuppa." She was recovered now and, once again, the thoughtful hostess.

After she'd gone Nicholas explained, "Me mum 'as t' go out lookin' fer sewin'." Katie understood that the woman needed work in order to support herself and her son.

Nicholas went on, "I wish she'd let us go look fer job 'stead a 'er, 'cause she's no' strong. But, she won' let us go ou' much," his brow wrinkled as if trying hard not to show his emotions. "She's afeard us'll get in wif that Pod an' 'is bunch," he muttered with deep feeling. "'N' she's afeard o' 'orses. She's afeard us'll git killed." It seemed he was lost in thought for a moment, before suddenly remembering he had guests. "Mum said I should fix cuppa." And he went to put a kettle on the hot stove.

When Nicholas returned with the teapot, a milk jug, and three cups on a tray, he asked a lot of questions about Peggy, her size, her colour, and her strength.

"I 'eard in street that thieves 're stealin' ponies and shipping them norf to be pit ponies in mines." He said he wouldn't put it past Pod and his gang to have stolen the little horse to sell to the men who supplied the mines.

"They sez on street tha' strong young ponies bring lot o' brass," he said. "Mines are far away in the norf. They need small 'orses t' fit in tunnels, but strong-like fer work. In dark," he added almost as an afterthought. "'Erd they live 'ole lives undergroun', and mos' goes blind wif no light."

"Blind! And so far away!" exclaimed Katie. She couldn't control her emotion any longer. Her face crumpled.

"'Ere, 'ere," said Nicholas, gently. "Jist be glad yer no' a lad. Laws bin changed, but it don' stop th' bad uns." He explained that while child labour was now illegal, there were still greedy mine owners who used children to work in the mines, so in addition to ponies being stolen, boys were being kidnapped. He went on. "Yer pony wuz only jist took. She won' be far."

Katie took a deep breath and concentrated. "You think she's still near here somewhere? Oh, Nicholas," she pleaded, "please help us find her!"

It was plain that a struggle was going on in the boy's mind. On the one hand, his mother didn't want him to stray far from home. And for good reason, Katie thought, with all those ruffians out there. On the other hand, he was kind and considerate and wanted to help.

Nicholas suddenly spoke briskly, as if he'd made a decision. "Us've been watching out window fer Pod 'n 'is gang fer weeks now. They jist cime back. They'll be robbin' folks and shops roun' 'ere fer few days—'til they're noticed by the Old Bill." He saw Katie's blank look. "Old Bill. You know, th' p'lice. Then they goes somewheres else. Me mum'll be 'ome soon. It's 'mos' tea time so we can't do nuthin' t'day. But you come in mornin', dress dark-like, 'n' us'll find 'em, don' worry."

But Katie was worried. Where was Peggy? The good little pony, always so patient and comforting when Katie told her her troubles, might be suffering right now at the hands of those cruel boys. Peggy was her best friend, she knew now. Samantha obviously wasn't the perfect girl she'd imagined. But Peggy was always calm and understanding. Just the thought of Peggy's plight devastated her. Once again, she lost control. She burst into tears and didn't stop until she was behind Samantha, on Jimbo's back, riding home.

Katie was so deep in thought about poor Peggy that she was almost back at the house before she wondered what Samantha's parents would say about the girls going to the East End and of her pony being stolen.

"Don't worry about them," said Samantha. "I'll take care of everything."

Samantha told Billy that they had left Peggy at a friend's house and to please not tell Papa or any of the house staff. Billy looked stern and disapproving.

"Er y' girlies up t' somethin'?" he asked.

Samantha looked at him with wide-eyed innocence. "Now, Billy, whatever would make you think that? And Billy," she said, dropping her voice, "I remember that you asked me not to tell Papa about your, your little secret."

Billy looked startled. Then, after a moment's thought, he grinned and winked. "I c'n keep secret if y' c'n."

When they were alone, Samantha told Katie, "Once I caught Billy smoking in the back of the barn. Papa has a fear of fire—there have been some terrible fires in London—so he strictly forbids anyone to smoke in the stable. It's full of dried hay and old straw and could go up with the tiniest spark.

"Billy begged me not to tell Papa what he'd been doing, saying he was ever so careful and always kept a bucket of water at hand as he smoked. I agreed to keep his secret, and now," she said with a toss of her head, "I'm glad I did."

Katie wasn't shocked that Samantha used blackmail against Billy to get what she wanted. Nothing about Samantha shocked her anymore. She longed, with all her heart, to find Peggy. And she longed for her dear little Peggy to take her home.

—Chapter 13—
Rescue

The next morning Katie and Samantha dressed in dark riding clothes and black boots, and rode Jimbo bareback to the East End. After they had tethered him to the post they met Nicholas at his flat. He asked them in and explained that he was alone. His mother was at the orphanage "askin' fer sewin'." Nicholas wore black trousers and a black jacket. Katie guessed that his mother had cut them down from much larger ones, probably clothes that had once belonged to his father.

Nicholas had everything planned. "W'en us saw Pod 'n gang from window, they came 'n went up street. They come back 'ere jist arter us woke, t' w'ere they stole pony, t' steal more, Oi reckon. Us figured their 'idin' place be nearby. We'll look fer 'ideout t'day."

"You're likely right. Perhaps Pod will come back here and lead us to his hideout so we'll find Peggy," said Katie, clapping her hands in anticipation.

The girls quickly agreed to put the plan into action. The three went to where Jimbo was tethered and hid in the dark shadows of an abandoned building. The girls couldn't see Jimbo, but Nicholas stood around the corner from them where he could easily see anyone who approached.

Just as Samantha turned to Katie to say something, Nicholas's palm appeared at the corner of the building, fingers waggling, signalling them to be still. Katie and Samantha held their breath. They heard running feet far off but getting closer. They heard a man shouting in anger, then raucous laughter. Then the gang, Pod in the lead, flashed into their line of vision on the next street, the high street. Their pockets were bulging. The shouting man came into view running behind them. Katie couldn't make out what he was saying, but it was pretty clear he'd been robbed.

Nicholas motioned the girls to join him as he set off to follow the man. There were many pedestrians in the high street. The three jog-trotted to keep up. The man was rather stout and was falling ever further behind the gang. He had stopped shouting now and was gasping for air.

The man gave up and turned toward them. Nicholas, Samantha, and Katie suddenly slowed to a walk. The man didn't look up as they passed. His face was red. "Thievin' rotten young jackanapes," he muttered angrily to himself, as he strode back the way he had come.

As soon as he was past, Nicholas started to trot again. "Los' sight o' Pod 'n' gang," he said as the girls joined him. "Let's find 'em." Katie scanned the street and gasped. Coming out from between some buildings a little ahead of them were Pod and his gang, walking in the same direction they were. The boys were talking and jostling among themselves and didn't look back.

Nicholas had spotted them, too. "Act like yer on yer own," he told the girls. "Follow behind like so it won' look like yur wif us."

With Nicholas in the lead, they followed the gang a couple of blocks, then Pod signalled a halt and looked behind him. Katie's breath caught in her throat. Samantha suddenly squatted, fixing a bootlace, so Katie nonchalantly looked into a shop window. She turned her head slightly to see Nicholas standing a block ahead looking bewildered, as if Pod and his gang had disappeared once more. Nicholas disappeared from view for a moment as a hawker with a cart turned at the intersection behind him.

Katie hastily turned her gaze back to the shop window. Inside was a display of bolts of cloth. As she peered at them, trying to figure out their next move, she realized that the window was acting as a mirror.

In the glass was the reflection of people walking by, then a team of horses and a wagon passing. She thought it was safe now, so she turned her back to the shop when, just by chance, she saw Pod reflected in a shop window across the street. He and his gang were crossing the street at the corner. She grasped Samantha's hand and said, "Come on. We might lose them." She pointed at the gang rapidly being swallowed up in the crowd. Samantha held back, not wanting to go without Nicholas, who was still hidden from them. Katie was thinking of Peggy and set off on her own across the street so she wouldn't lose sight of the young thieves.

By the time she finally got across the mud and the ruts, dodging horses and wheels, she looked up the street and down, but couldn't see the gang. They had vanished into thin air. When Nicholas and Samantha caught up with her, Katie was beside herself. She was tired, she was hungry, and she still didn't know where Peggy was. Nicholas said, "Sorry, Kitie, wish we could've foun' pony. Me mum'll be 'ome an' she'll worry 'bout us ef we're gone. Us 'ave t' go 'ome now."

"I think we should all go home and try again tomorrow," said Samantha. Katie had the impression that Samantha wouldn't stay without Nicholas. Peggy just wasn't that important to her.

Katie didn't want to leave. She desperately wanted to find her pony but she knew she couldn't stay in the East End on her own. "Oh, all right," she said. "As long as you both promise to come back here tomorrow."

Nicholas readily agreed. Once he had Samantha's assurance that she knew her way, he hurried off home to his mother. The girls were slowly walking toward Jimbo's post when Pod's gang suddenly came careening across the street in front of them. "Samantha, look!" said Katie, suddenly energized. It looked like another theft, with an irate victim chasing the thieves. In their headlong rush to escape capture, the boys bumped into a woman, knocking her down, scattering her parcels. Several people went to her aid. In the midst of the confusion, the girls were able to follow the boys unnoticed. Once again, they had to run to keep up, but this time the boys didn't stop to look behind them. They ran straight to a dark, narrow alleyway.

The gang stopped in front of a derelict shed. Katie and Samantha ducked out of sight as Pod scanned the alley to make sure they hadn't been followed. Reassured, he stepped up to the door and said softly, "Open up. Ef yez know wot's good fer yer, yer'll open." The door swung outward with a rusty groan and the boys filed in, shutting the door behind them. Katie and Samantha silently approached the shed.

"I wish Nicholas was still here," said Samantha quietly. "He'd know what to do next."

"Sh," said Katie. "Let's find out what's going on. Maybe Peggy's in there." Her heart was pounding.

Samantha followed Katie as she tiptoed around to the back of the building. There were small boarded-up windows where they might have found a crack to peek through, but they were high above their heads. Katie scanned the wall, and noticed some boards that had shrunk over the years. There was a half-inch crack, just wide enough for one person to peek inside.

"Let me see," whispered Samantha, pushing past Katie. Katie

waited a minute or two, but couldn't wait any longer. She pulled her friend's sleeve to remind her it was her turn. Only then did the older girl grudgingly let her look through the crack.

It took a few seconds to adjust to the dimness, but Katie could see the boys sitting in a circle around a lantern. An array of goods was spread within the circle on the floor. Katie could make out men's pocket watches, a scattering of coins, and a few ladies' handbags. The boys were emptying bags onto the pile. Pod was busy counting money.

The boys were whispering among themselves. Then Katie heard what she'd been listening for. A faint nicker. Peggy! Katie was flooded with relief. Perhaps Peggy could sense Katie on the other side of the wall, for she nickered again. Katie held her breath, but the boys didn't look up from their spoils.

Pod finally rose to his feet and spoke to someone outside the circle of light. Katie couldn't see a face. She heard Pod say, "... 'll come by to pick up pony at tea time." Pod suddenly reached out, grabbed the hidden person, and dragged him over to the circle. Katie could now see a boy about the same age as Pod, probably in his late teens, but a taller, heavier young man. He must have been inside all the time, Katie realized.

"Oi'm warnin' ya, Rats," growled Pod, "us knows 'ow much brass'll be in package, an' if ye tike any, m' lads'll give ya roit thrashin'. Roit mites?"

Rats was literally shaking in his boots. From what Katie had heard, Pod was known for his cruelty. Rats's terrified voice rose in pitch as he spoke. "Us promises t' stop roit 'ere 'til us gets brass, an' us'll stop 'til y' comes fer it."

Pod muttered something Katie couldn't hear, then he and his gang left the building. When they reached the street they let loose joyous shouts and laughter which carried back into the alleyway. No wonder they're happy, thought Katie. They've made quite a haul today.

Katie pulled Samantha deeper into the alley before she felt safe enough to tell her about Peggy. "I'm sure she's in there. I heard her. We have to get her out, and quickly. Pod said they'd come to get Peggy at tea time. When's that?"

Samantha explained, "Tea time is what they call the evening meal around here. Usually around six o'clock."

It was about two o'clock. And the guard in the barn, the one called Rats, had promised he wouldn't leave until Pod came back. They had to think of a way to get the pony out from under Rats's nose.

Katie came up with a plan. "Samantha, I want you to provide a distraction to get Rats out of the shed while I sneak in and get Peggy."

Her desire for adventure taking over, Samantha eagerly agreed. She walked boldly around the shed. Suddenly she fell in a heap, moaning loudly. "Help," she wailed. "Oh, my ankle!"

As she peeked around the corner, Katie realized how amateurish this ruse was. Would Rats leave valuable stolen goods unattended to help some stranger? Not likely.

Katie knew what might get him outside. She stepped back from the building and shouted loudly: "I hear you, Miss. You just wait there and I'll bring a policeman!"

It seemed the word policeman was barely out of her mouth when the young giant burst out the door. "No need fer th' Old Bill. Oi'll help ya t' shop on 'igh street, an' someone there 'll take y' 'ome."

He offered Samantha a hand, and Katie saw her hobble away

down the lane, holding on to his arm as if her life depended on it.

As soon as they were out of sight, Katie ran into the shed. The lantern was still lit, hanging on a post. She smelled the warm horse smell before she could make out Peggy in the gloom. But Peggy wasn't alone. Another pony, brown-coloured and a little bigger than Peggy, was tied beside her. No wonder the thieves were happy. They had two ponies to sell to the mines!

Luckily Peggy's bridle and saddle had been thrown on the floor beside her. Katie had her ready in a blink. She scrambled onto Peggy's back, and was ducking out the doorway when Rats came running toward them.

"Thief! 'Orse thief!" he shouted. Katie laughed and shouted back, "I'm just taking back my own property." As he reached a ham hand to grab the bridle, Katie leaned down and whispered in Peggy's ear. Peggy reared. Rats jumped backward to avoid flailing hooves, and Peggy galloped past him, down the lane, to the open street.

Samantha was just ahead on Jimbo, ready to go. Katie glanced over her shoulder, but all she could see was a street filled with horses, carriages, wagons, and pedestrians trying to pick their way among them. The girls turned into a quieter street where they were able to bring their horses to a gallop. Then they heard galloping hooves behind them. They turned to see Rats following them on the brown pony. He looked ridiculous with his big body hunched over the pony's shoulders, and his long legs hanging low on either side. His pony was surprisingly fleet, and with every bound it was getting closer.

With Katie still struggling to ride sidesaddle and Samantha riding Jimbo bareback, the girls' mounts weren't as fast as their pursuer's pony. They were getting closer to home and safety, but would they be able to get there before they were caught? In her fear, Katie could visualize Rats pulling her to the ground and leaving her, bleeding, while he stole Peggy away. And she would never see her pony again!

She leaned forward, desperate to escape. Samantha, in the lead, swung into the park where they had taken their exercise yesterday. Katie was heartened, for this was a shortcut to Billy and safety. But her heart sank when she realized it was a mistake. For some strange reason, the park was empty. No one to call to for help. No one to report the attack and theft that was coming any minute.

Ahead of her, Samantha and Jimbo thundered down the hard-packed bridle path. Peggy, carrying Katie, followed as fast as her short little legs could go. Hard on their heels was Rats, free of restrictive clothing, free of saddle, free to send his pony into a lather of speed, getting ever closer.

Just as Katie was certain Rats was in arm's reach, Peggy made a little jump in the air, and she and Katie were soaring in the wind.

Rats pulled up quickly, his amazed face turned up toward them. Samantha let out a cheer and slowed Jimbo. She knew Rats wasn't interested in her or her horse. She watched Katie on her magical pony, soaring upward to the sky, high above the park, far from danger.

—Chapter 14—
Home Again

From the time Peggy slowly circled Haggarty's pasture and brought Katie back to earth, it was as if they had never been away. Katie landed in her own clothes, riding bareback. When she got home, Mom said, "Katie, now that the horses are taken care of, would you please peel some apples for dessert?" Clearly, time in the Yukon had stood still. In her mother's mind, she'd only been away long enough to do her chores at Haggarty's. There was no mention of her storming out.

Katie didn't know what to make of it all. She'd expected her parents' joy at her return, but they had no idea she'd been gone. She had come back to her old life of pain and confusion. In contrast, Samantha's home had been filled with order and tranquility. Despite her frightening run-ins with Pod's gang and Peggy being stolen, she had found her time in Samantha's home to be happy, like her life before the move, before Siggi. As soon as she stepped inside the door of the cramped little cabin she despised, and saw Siggi, that happiness disappeared. Somehow, Katie resented her parents all the more, felt their betrayal more keenly. She desperately wanted to return to London, but when she rode Peggy in the ensuing days, the mare showed no inclination to fly.

Katie didn't say a word about time-travelling. No one would believe her. Besides, her parents were so wrapped up with Siggi, they didn't even care about her.

Katie got a surprise when she first returned home and opened her Victorian doll box. There it was, right on top. The Samantha doll. First she thought Siggi must have been scared of getting caught with it so had sneaked it back into her room while she was out. But the more she thought about it, the more she doubted this simple explanation. She had to admit that Siggi didn't show any signs of guilt and he didn't seem secretive. That night, as she was on the edge of sleep, another explanation popped into her mind. She sat up in bed with the shock of it.

Katie was sure she knew why the doll was back. The magnetic doll was her link with Samantha and the nineteenth century. The doll had disappeared before, just before she had met Samantha in the flesh. Now the real Samantha was beyond reach and the doll was back. When the doll was gone, Samantha was present. When the doll was here, Samantha was gone. It all became so clear. The reappearance of the doll now strengthened Katie's fear that the real girl was gone, forever this time.

After an hour of gut-wrenching contemplation, Katie settled down into a fitful sleep. As she drifted off, a thought nagged at her. Maybe because she resented her parents so much for bringing Siggi into the family without consulting her, she'd been too quick to jump to the conclusion that he'd taken the doll. It was possible that Siggi had been innocent all along.

She was still upset in the morning. She longed to escape to Samantha's home again. She opened the box where she kept the dolls. Samantha was not there!

After a big weekend breakfast, she said something about helping Mr. Haggarty and ran outside before her parents could reply. She needed Peggy, her other connection to Samantha's world.

The little mare was drowsing in her stall. Katie threw her arms around her neck and poured out her feelings. She stood there, soaking in the peace of the barn and the understanding of her beloved pony. Then she heard a rumble.

The barn door slid about a foot before it got stuck. Katie ran to help, thinking it might be one of the other horse-owners. But it was Siggi.

"Dad says you have to give me a ride." His face was hot and rosy from running. She looked down at him. Right now he looked so small. Pity stirred in her once again.

"I might give you a ride," she said, "but first you have to tell me the truth. Did you take my Samantha doll?" She needed to know if her theory was correct, or if Siggi really was the cause of the doll's disappearance.

He looked up at her with his pale eyes unblinking. "Honest, Katie, I didn't touch it."

This time she believed he was telling the truth. The doll's disappearance didn't have anything to do with Siggi at all; it was simply part of the magic. Its disappearance today must mean... a little bird of hope fluttered in her heart.

"Oh, come on then," she said, feeling she had to make up for her false accusations. "I'll take you for a ride, but it's going to be short!" She wasn't prepared to be overly generous.

With Siggi behind her, snuggled against her back, she let Peggy have her head. Siggi didn't know how to ride properly so this was taking a chance. If Peggy trotted and jiggled he might slide off. A little beast inside her wanted that to happen. If he fell off and hurt himself, he'd never bother her about riding Peggy again.

Peggy didn't seem to notice the extra weight of the second rider. She trotted, shaking her head and rattling her bridle, happy to be outside in the fresh, crisp air. Siggi gripped Katie's waist tightly so he didn't slide.

Suddenly Peggy slipped from a trot to a gallop, then into her smooth fifth gait. Siggi laughed out loud. Katie could feel the side of his face against her back.

It wasn't until the pressure left her back and she heard Siggi gasp that Katie realized they'd left the earth. They were soaring through the sky with the silent wind rushing past them. The stars hanging large and bright.

"Wow," breathed Siggi.

Oh no! Siggi was flying with her! Katie had to think fast. "Yes, Peggy can fly," she said. "This has to be our secret, okay? Mom and Dad wouldn't understand. You know they wouldn't, Siggi."

But Siggi was excited. He wasn't ready to promise anything. "Katie, I never knew your pony could fly! Wow, the sky's so beautiful! You'll take me with you when you go out riding again, won't you?"

When Katie didn't answer, he played his trump card. "If you don't take me when the pony flies, I'll tell on you!"

She didn't know how to respond to this. She felt sure that if she were in Siggi's place, she'd want to fly just as badly, so she didn't blame him. But he was forcing her to take him riding on her magical pony. He was worming his way in on this special, private part of her life. But, if she didn't take him and he told her parents, how would she possibly explain Peggy's flights to them? She could deny what he said, but they always took his side over hers.

Katie was relieved when Peggy started the slow circling of her descent. Maybe, once they were back on solid ground, she could convince Siggi it had never happened. That he had imagined the whole thing.

Peggy hit earth with a little bump and started trotting again. Katie's first inkling of disaster was when she realized they hadn't landed behind Haggarty's barn. She heard the clop of Peggy's hooves on cobblestones. Thick yellowish fog enveloped them, and she could hear familiar sounds: the shouts of a man manoeuvring his horses through the crowded streets, the whinny of a horse pulling a carriage, its wheels clattering on the cobbles.

Katie was horrified. She was back in nineteenth-century England. And, accidentally, she had done a terrible and frightening thing. She had brought Siggi with her.

Peggy took them to Samantha's house. Billy stared at Siggi, no doubt trying to figure out who this child might be. Katie stared at Siggi, too, for he was now dressed in below-the-knee trousers and a tight, collarless jacket. Billy didn't say a word as he took Peggy by the bridle to lead her to her stall. Ever since Samantha had threatened him with telling his secret, he hadn't interfered in any of the girls' escapades. Siggi was stunned into silence. He clung to Katie's hand as they walked through the back garden toward the house.

In the warm, steamy kitchen, Daisy rushed out of the scullery with a big basin of peeled potatoes. She was about to put them into a pot of boiling water next to Cook who was basting a huge joint of beef resting in a black pan on the open oven door, when they both noticed Katie and Siggi.

"Ay up! Wot's this?" said Cook. Then she turned to Daisy. "You tike ker of this right smart or I'll know reason why," and she went back to her roast.

Daisy gave a frightened look toward Cook's back, and whisked Katie and Siggi into the scullery where they could talk privately.

"Ee then, wot's a boy doin' 'ere?"

She didn't ask where Katie had been; indeed, she didn't seem aware that Katie had been gone. But Katie had Daisy's question to contend with. She had learned from Samantha how to avoid awkward questions. You ignored them.

"Where's Samantha?" she asked, echoing Samantha's imperious tone. "Tell her I must speak with her immediately."

Daisy deferred to the tone of authority. "I'll get 'er fer y', Miss. She jist got back from park. I reckons she's in nursery wi' little 'uns." And, most amazingly, Daisy dropped a curtsey before she dashed off, just as if Katie had a right to order her around.

Katie turned toward Siggi. "You're going to meet my friend, Samantha. She is a real live girl, not a doll. She's part of the magic," she explained.

Siggi looked around open-mouthed. Then he looked down at his clothes, but he still said nothing.

Samantha was, for a moment, stunned to see Katie back so soon, and this time with a small boy, who looked, for all the world, like another little brother. "Let's take him up to the morning room to meet my parents. What's his name again?"

When Katie reminded her of Siggi's name, Samantha chuckled. Katie was appalled at her rudeness and hoped Siggi hadn't been offended, but then remembered that she had once found Siggi's name very strange, too. Perhaps her attitude to Siggi was changing. She decided to ignore Samantha's rudeness.

"Perhaps we should take him up to our bedroom first to have him practice answering the questions your parents will ask," Katie suggested.

"All right then. Follow me," ordered Samantha.

They sat on Samantha's bed, like three birds on a fence. Siggi looked at the velvet curtains on the windows, the metal bedstead decorated with intricate white-painted scrolls, and once again at his clothes.

The girls quizzed him until his answers were letter perfect. After the girls were through with him, he seemed quite accepting of the strange circumstances. Katie knew from her own experience that after riding a flying pony, nothing here seemed that strange. He accepted the fact that they had to be secretive. He even got quite excited at one point and said, "This is fun!"

"Siggi," ordered Samantha. "Pay attention and do as I say. This is your final chance to practice your answers. Who are you and why are you here?"

"I'm Katie's little brother," answered Siggi in a singsong voice. Katie squirmed uncomfortably, but squelched the feeling. She and Samantha had agreed that was the simplest explanation. "I came to England with her on a ship. While Katie came to London to visit relatives, I stayed with our great uncle in Portsmouth. Uncle brought me down to London, and we saw Katie and Samantha in the park. Uncle left me with them, er, you..." Siggi stopped in confusion but Katie was nodding encouragingly so he went on. "Then Uncle rushed off 'cause he had business to take care of. We waited and waited but he didn't come back so you brought me here." The child was speaking so rapidly by the end of his speech, that he was almost incomprehensible. Katie and Samantha laughed, but they were both pleased that he could recite all this without a mistake.

Katie realized what a smart little boy Siggi was; he learned so quickly. Still, she was worried. The story they'd concocted was unbelievable. She couldn't think anyone would fall for it. But Samantha insisted that her parents wouldn't question it.

Samantha was right. Her parents seemed so engrossed in their own lives that they didn't take time to question the story, or even to think much about it. They were essentially good-hearted people, and if this child needed a home until his relatives appeared, then they would willingly provide it, just as they had for his sister. Katie thought of her own parents and their kindness to Siggi. Funny, she had never before thought of their taking him in as being anything but a selfish act.

Siggi was sent to the nursery where he would eat his meals with Nanny and the boys, and where he would sleep on a cot. Katie was concerned at first. Siggi was too young to have read anything about the period and he didn't have the background knowledge that she had gleaned from her book on Victorian England. As it turned out, she needn't have worried. Everyone assumed Siggi's ignorance was the result of his being from Canada. They all seemed to think Canada quite barbaric, so it was understandable that he ate with the wrong fork at their first meal together. Nanny took it upon herself to teach this ignorant child from the wilds, and patiently repeated her lessons when he made mistakes.

On his first morning in London, Siggi went to the park with Nanny and the boys. Samantha insisted that she and Katie take advantage of the situation and go to the East End to see Nicholas. "We have to let him know we got Peggy back," she explained. Katie was nervous about going. She was afraid of running into Pod and his gang, and she was afraid for Peggy's safety. But Samantha was so insistent, she finally relented.

As they made their way, Katie turned often to look over her shoulder. She refused to leave Peggy tethered with Jimbo around the corner from the Campers' shop until Samantha hired a hawker, a woman selling violets from a barrow, to guard the horses for half an hour. When the girls reached Nicholas's flat, they were alarmed to discover a padlock on the door. When they stood back and looked up to the front windows, there were no curtains.

They hurried to the shop window and looked in. The boots were gone! A neighbour woman explained, "The bailiffs come yistidy an' pu' 'em out."

"Where did they go?" asked Katie.

The woman shrugged.

Reluctantly the girls left the street and rode home. They had a new worry. Where was Nicholas? Was he safe?

Chapter 15
Searching for Nicholas

The girls searched for Nicholas for weeks with no luck. He seemed to have disappeared from the face of the earth. Katie was very concerned. The days were getting shorter and colder. Were Nicholas and his mother dry and warm?

In the Yukon, short days meant winter was on its way, bringing clean, white snow. Winter came later in England. When it did come, it snowed, but the snow quickly became dirty and lay in dark ragged banks at the side of the streets. The foul-smelling fogs were heavier than ever. It was usually damp and chill but there were also sharp cold snaps with frost. Everybody was complaining about the worst winter in years. Samantha didn't seem to know how to take the cold. "I'm not used to this," she said. Katie, on the other hand, expected freezing temperatures and accepted the cold snaps as normal.

Katie hated the bother of putting on extra clothing when there was no fun to be had playing in the snow or skating on a rink. Winter in London was dark and unpleasant, not fun. But at least she was warm and dry in Samantha's house where there was plenty of coal for the fireplaces and the big black cooker, which kept the kitchen cozy. What about Nicholas and his mother? She hoped they were somewhere comfortable.

Siggi didn't seem to mind the unpleasant weather. Life here was full of fun for him, no matter what it was like outside. He enjoyed

playing with Wilbur, Samantha's brother, and accepted his surroundings as if it was the most natural thing in the world for a
twenty-first-century child to journey to another time. He acted
like a bratty little brother to Katie and Samantha and he ignored
two-year-old Elbert as beneath his contempt because he was still
a baby "in skirts."

Siggi and Wilbur were always getting into mischief. One day
they found a hibernating grass snake, took it out of its hollow log,
and put it in Cook's breadbox. When she lifted the lid, her scream
could be heard clear up to the nursery. The boys rolled on the
floor, laughing 'til tears ran down their cheeks. Katie and Samantha, getting ready for lessons, rolled their eyes and muttered
about immature children.

Katie was feeling increasingly homesick. She was beginning to
think that Samantha's family wasn't so perfect after all. Samantha's parents only spent time with their children during the reading time that followed the evening meal. By comparison, Mom
and Dad spent hours each day with her and Siggi, even though
both had busy, full-time jobs. She missed them terribly.

Once, when she had a moment alone with Siggi, she said, "Siggi,
I want you to come riding with me today. We should try to get
Peggy to take us home to the Yukon."

"I don't want to go back," said Siggi. "I like it better here. You're
not as mean as you are at home."

Katie couldn't argue with him. It was true. It was easier to be
nice to him here, for some reason. When Samantha referred to
him as Katie's little brother, it no longer bothered her as it had
when they first arrived. She hoped that, eventually, Siggi would
change his mind. Someday he'd want to go home, too. Home.
Katie realized that she was thinking it was Siggi's home as well as

hers.

There was another reason that Katie didn't argue with Siggi about staying. Although she missed her parents, she had a feeling that as long as Nicholas was missing, she needed to stay and finish her search.

Christmas preparations were under way in the kitchen. First, Cook made mincemeat for pies. "Smells like Christmas, don't it?" said Daisy.

With the mincemeat out of the way, Cook's next job was to make plum pudding. She stirred raisins, dates, and candied peel into the stiff dough. It was hard work and sweat broke out on her forehead. "'Ere," she said, "you girlies each 'ave a stir—fer luck." While the girls were stirring, Cook busied herself washing coins in hot water, then she threw the freshly cleaned money in the batter.

"Why on earth are you doing that?" asked Katie. But Cook just gave her a mysterious look and refused to answer.

When Christmas cards arrived in "the post," Siggi asked Wilbur's mother if he could look at them. He went to the window for better light and stared at the pictures of Father Christmas with his white beard and red robe. The first time carollers came to the door singing the old familiar Christmas songs, he got very excited. Siggi and Wilbur were allowed to pass out hot little mincemeat pies and a small cup of Christmas punch to each singer as a way of saying thank you.

Katie, on the other hand, was very homesick. She'd never been away from her parents at Christmas; all the preparations made her long for home. When Siggi finished with the Christmas cards, she looked at them, too, but not at Father Christmas. She stared at the sleighs pulled by prancing horses through snow. Snow! She missed the crisp cold, the white fields sparkling in the moonlight, the stars dancing above her in the frosty air. She missed Canada. She missed the Yukon. She missed her mom and dad.

Christmas Eve arrived and still Samantha and Katie had not found Nicholas. They set off to look once more. "I hope he's able to celebrate Christmas, wherever he is," said Katie.

Samantha looked at her with a kind of pitying look. Then she explained, "The lower classes don't celebrate Christmas. To Mother James, and street urchins like Pod, this is just another day. To Nicholas and his mother, though, it's a special religious day." Katie was quite surprised to hear this. As far as she knew, there wasn't a class system in modern-day Canada where the rich celebrated Christmas while the poor didn't. It seemed quite unfair to her.

The girls' mounts trotted down the slushy high street. They were going through an intersection when Peggy stopped suddenly and shook her bridle in fear. She had collided with a tall man crossing the street. As the unfortunate pedestrian regained his feet and bent to wipe off his clothes, Katie saw it wasn't a man. "Mother James!" she shouted. The woman looked up at Katie, who was sure she saw a glimmer of recognition, but turned quickly away and didn't answer. Strange, thought Katie. She leaned forward to whisper soothing words to her spooked little horse. From the corner of her eye, she could see the big rangy woman with the red nose and strange topknot stagger a bit before continuing her way down the street, carrying a large covered basket.

Katie and Samantha exchanged looks. Mother James hadn't been shy with words the first time they'd met. She'd obviously been drinking now, but she'd been drinking then, too. Why was she hurrying then stopping every once in a while to look over her shoulder?

"She looks guilty," said Katie.

"I wonder what she's up to?" said Samantha. "Let's follow her."

Samantha stopped at a hitching post in front of a shop. "We can't follow inconspicuously as long as we're mounted," she said.

"I absolutely refuse to leave Peggy," said Katie.

Samantha gave her an exasperated glare, then looked around.

"You there," she barked at a neatly dressed boy nearby. "Why are you standing there gawking?"

Katie was embarrassed by Samantha's rudeness. She smiled sympathetically at the boy behind her friend's back, then turned to keep an eye on Mother James.

"I'm waitin' for me mam who's buyin' new frock," the boy answered.

"If she's like my mother, you'll be here a long wait," said Samantha. "Keep an eye on these horses. If they're here when we get back, you'll be well paid." She jangled the coins in her purse.

The horses taken care of, the girls were free to follow Mother James. They were still able to see the woman's topknot over the heads of the people in front of them. Mother James couldn't see the girls in her frequent over-the-shoulder checks, for they were shorter than most of the crowd. They followed her from a discreet distance. There were fewer pedestrians now and the girls ducked into doorways whenever Mother James slowed her headlong pace, as she did each time she took another look over her shoulder. She seemed to relax after a while when she still hadn't spotted them. The girls were quite far back now, but watching intently. When Mother James crossed an intersection, a horse and wagon blocked her from view for a few moments. Katie took a quick look around. The surroundings looked familiar.

When she looked back to where she'd last seen Mother James,

she caught a glimpse of the big woman disappearing into an alleyway. Katie knew where they were now. Mother James was leading
them back to where Pod and his gang had held Peggy captive.

The girls peeked around the corner in time to see the woman
disappear into the shack's dark doorway.

"Let's see what there is to see," Samantha whispered.

They found the crack where they'd watched before. This time
Katie asked Samantha if she could look first. Samantha reluctantly
agreed. When Katie could see nothing, she pressed her ear to it.

She could hear Mother James talking. "I've brung ya somethin'
ta eat," the big woman said in her gravelly voice. "I brung ya what
y'arsked fer."

"An' 'ere's yer pay," answered a familiar voice—Pod's. "This be
nuff t' buy ya jug o' that gin ya likes t' guzzle." Katie heard the
clink of coins and a grunt of approval from Mother James.

"An' there's more where that come from," said Pod. "Effen you
bring us lads, smallish like, there'll be lotsa brass fer ya."

"Lads? Got one lad," she said. "'most an orphan. Da's planted,
ma's goin' soon."

"'Ow old?"

"Near twelve."

"Too big. Seven or eight 'bout roit," said Pod.

"Can get coupla small lads, 'bout seven years," said Mother
James.

"Awroit," said Pod.

"C'n bring ya lotsa small lads," she said.

"Us'll start wi' two," Pod said violently. There was silence for a
moment then the woman's voice came from the direction of the
door. She said, "Oi 'ave t' git to m' bairns. Oi'll be back t' talk
'nother toim."

Pod just grunted, so the woman left, clinking the coins in her pocket.

Katie looked at Samantha and motioned her to follow. Samantha obediently tiptoed behind her until they were out of hearing of those in the shed. Katie told her friend what she'd heard.

"Mother James said she had a twelve-year-old. Do you think it could be Nicholas? I think we should go to her place and find out," said Katie.

"It's one place we haven't looked," said Samantha. "Let's go!"

The door to Mother James's house was ajar. Samantha pushed it open and the girls went silently into the dim hallway. They could hear Mother James's loud voice, but it wasn't coming from the dingy room where she lived. It was coming from the room next to it.

"Listen up. Yer feelin' sick, 'n' I c'n 'elp," she was saying in a wheedling tone. "Oi'll go t' market an' git food in 'n' charge next to nuthin' fer m' trouble."

Katie and Samantha crept silently through the dim hallway. Any noise could bring an angry Mother James out to investigate, and Katie was terrified of what she might do. The girls stopped in the shadows across from the open door, but still couldn't see who the woman was speaking to. All they could see through the door was a smoke-darkened wall, a patch of damp, and some pieces of plaster hanging from the ceiling. They could hear a woman coughing. She was trying to speak, but the effort made her cough as if she would choke.

A frightened child's voice spoke. "Ta, Mother James. That's roit kind, but me mum 'n' me don' 'ave the brass." The girls recognized that voice. Nicholas! At last, they'd found him.

Mother James's mood changed completely. "Ef ya don' 'ave

brass fer m' 'elp," she hollered, "bes' gimme brass fer room—now, or it's out on street wi' bof a ya."

As soon as the woman had begun to yell, Katie and Samantha made a dash for the door. They had just slipped through when an enraged Mother James stomped into the hallway and through the door to her own room. The girls hid outside, hoping Mother James would leave so they could speak to Nicholas, but no such luck. They knew they couldn't wait any longer; they had to get back for Christmas Eve with Samantha's family.

Once they were safely back on their horses, Katie said, "Do you think Nicholas has been there all this time? I wonder what that woman is up to. I wonder if the owner of the house knows she's collecting rent from the Campers."

They chattered all the way home. They were happy that they'd finally found Nicholas, but now they were worried about Mother James's threats.

When the girls got home, Daisy scolded them for being late on such an important night—Christmas Eve! The girls hurriedly washed and put on fresh clothes for supper.

When the meal was over, Samantha's parents took the children upstairs to the parlour, a special room most often used for important visitors. There the girls decorated a small tree with strings of popcorn and cranberries, then they clipped little candles to its branches. Because it was Christmas Eve, the parents devoted the evening to the children. The father played horsey on the floor with the little boys on his back, while Baby Elbert laughed and waved his rattle at them from a corner. The horsey pranced and whinnied and finally reared up on his knees. The little boys slid off in a tangle of laughter. Katie and Samantha talked quietly to each other as they waited patiently at the table to play checkers

with the parents. After the game, Samantha's mother played the
piano and they all sang carols.

Before Nanny came to take the small children upstairs to bed,
each child hung a stocking on the mantle for Father Christmas
to fill. Even the girls did this, though they were almost grown up.
Then Samantha's father lit the candles on the tree and turned off
the gaslights for a few minutes. It was a magical sight. As they all
gazed in wonder at the flickering lights, the sound of church bells
peeled joyously across the city. The magic of the night was com-
plete.

Tucked into their warm beds, the girls reviewed the day. They
had finally found Nicholas, but he was in danger of being turned
out of his home once again. And by listening in on Mother James
at the hideout, they had stumbled on something important, something sinister and frightening. They knew that two small boys
were about to be kidnapped, likely to be sold into slave labour for
the mines. Could they somehow prevent this terrible thing from
happening?

Katie fell asleep with church bells ringing in her ears, and
her heart aching to be with her parents again in her own home.
Christmas with Samantha's family made her more homesick than
ever. She drifted off while lovingly holding her locket, with its
picture of her family, next to her heart.

—Chapter 16—
The Plot

Katie's eyes fluttered open before dawn. Samantha was already up and dressed. Even though they crept downstairs in the dark, Siggi and Wilbur were there before them. The stockings were knobbly with oranges, candy, and small toys. Larger gifts were under the tree. Katie and Samantha each found a porcelain woman-doll dressed elaborately in silks and satins. Katie thought her doll was absolutely beautiful. Wilbur got a mechanical cart pulled by a toy goat, while Siggi was ecstatic over a hobby horse with a red bridle painted on its head. There was a Noah's Ark with pairs of animals for Elbert, who promptly stuffed a giraffe in his mouth and chewed on it. The children were busy with their gifts when the parents came into the room, tying the sashes on their robes and yawning.

Daisy served breakfast in the dining room at eight o'clock, then she and Cook went to their rooms to dress for church. When they came back from the service, they changed into work clothes and started preparing vegetables for Christmas dinner. While they were busy in the scullery and kitchen, the family went to church.

The children, sitting with Nanny behind the parents, had a hard time sitting still through the long, boring sermon. Nanny chastised Samantha for reading a book surreptitiously during the service. Katie had lots of time to worry about Nicholas. By the time they got home and Nanny had gone to her room, the roast goose, brown and crispy, was "resting" on a platter, ready for the family feast. Katie set aside her worries for an hour and enjoyed the dinner. Her favourite dish was the plum pudding. Cook brought it into the dining room doused with warm brandy, which Samantha's father set aflame. When Katie found a coin in her portion, everyone clapped. "It's good luck," said Samantha.

After the feast, they all pulled Christmas crackers which came apart with satisfying BANGs, revealing paper hats, sweets wrapped in coloured paper, and small tin toys.

Dinner over, the younger children went back to the parlour to play with their new toys. Samantha had given Katie a little money to buy books for the parents. The Mama and Papa read from their books, and the servants rested, except for Daisy who "walked out" with her "gentleman friend."

"He's not a real gentleman," said Samantha. "He's just a servant from the next street."

"He seems very nice to me," said Katie, exasperated with Samantha's snobbery.

Samantha judged people unfairly. It had felt good to stand up for Daisy and her beau. Katie thought of Mad who was also judged unfairly. Katie vowed to do something about that, if she ever got home again.

With everyone occupied, it was easy for Samantha and Katie to get away for a ride. They headed right to Mother James's house, hoping Nicholas and his mother would still be there, and praying that Mother James would be out.

The girls let themselves in then waited in the sour-smelling hall, listening for Mother James's gravelly voice. All they heard was the crying of the baby and the scuffling sounds of the older children busy making brushes. Then someone opened the front door. The girls cowered in the gloom, but it was not Mother James, as they'd feared. Entering the house with a brisk, no-nonsense manner was a small woman in a sensible dress of grey with a matching bonnet. She didn't notice the girls but walked directly to the Campers' door and knocked. The door opened and they heard a pleased-sounding Nicholas say, "Miss Charity! Welcome."

Katie started toward the door, but Samantha grabbed her hand. "Let's wait 'til we find out who Miss Charity is," she whispered. Katie stopped, listening. They could hear Mrs. Camper coughing weakly. They could also hear the woman they called Miss Charity say she'd already been to the Christmas service, "but there's no rest for the wicked, so I must go on with my work today, even though it's Christmas. Especially since it's Christmas," she amended.

The door was left open a crack. Katie and Samantha crept silently toward it. They could now hear more clearly. "Nicholas, I know how much you hate begging in the streets, but I also know that your mother can't provide for you right now. So I've arranged for you to live in my orphanage. It's called Lost Lambs and it's quite well thought of. A bed has just become available and I'd like you to have it. You'll have nourishing food to eat and a clean bed to sleep in. And you'll learn a trade so your future will be brighter. Some of my luckier charges are given the opportunity of sailing to the colonies for more promising lives than they can find here."

"An orphanage?" said Mrs. Camper. "An' sendin' 'im away t' colonies? Oh, dear." Her voice was barely audible. "Nicholas isn't orphan. At least, not yet..." She fell into another coughing fit.

"Don't be fooled by the name, Mrs. Camper. Although most of the children at Lost Lambs are orphans, whenever there's space I take in those whose parents are unable to provide for them. You want what's best for Nicholas, don't you?"

"I won' go wi'out me mum," said Nicholas firmly.

"Not to worry! We'll get her out of this mould and damp. I've found a clean, dry room for your mother, and, once she is stronger, I'll continue to bring her sewing from the orphanage so she can earn money again."

There was a sound at the front door. The girls scurried back to their dark corner just in time to see Mother James thunder in and stagger to her room. They heard a few cries as she batted some of her unfortunate children. Apparently finding what she wanted, Mother James came out of her room, tucking a bottle of a colourless liquid into her boot top, then staggered out the door of the house. Katie knew she had to do something for those poor children. Miss Charity was the one to ask for help.

The moment Mother James was out of the house, the girls ran to the door of Nicholas's room. Katie knocked.

"Kitie! S'mantha! Wot wunnerful surprise!" Nicholas was clearly overjoyed to see them. He looked thinner. His mother looked very sick.

"Nicholas, we've been searching for you everywhere!" Samantha said as she gave him a big hug.

Katie hugged him, too, and smiled at his mother who was coughing so much she couldn't speak. Then, as Nicholas introduced them, she shook Miss Charity's hand. "Miss Charity, we need your help," she said once the pleasantries were over. Miss Charity listened intently as Katie told her about Mother James's children, and that she and Samantha had overheard the woman planning to abduct small boys and sell them.

"I wouldn't put it pas' 'er," said Nicholas. "All she kers fer is brass fer gin."

Miss Charity paced the floor as she spoke, her face full of concern. "I know you think I should intervene, Katie, but I can't. For one thing, I'm not sure Mother James's children are in immediate danger. It sounds like this treatment has been going on for some time. And the children do have a parent who keeps a roof over their heads—that's more than many have.

"Mother James is obviously addicted to gin," she continued. "But so are hundreds of unhappy parents in this cruel city. Gin is cheap and is often seen as the only way out of their troubles. I learned long ago that I can't help them all. Any investigation of this case will have to wait. As for allegations of a proposed abduction, you have no evidence other than something you've overheard."

Katie suppressed her feelings of frustration. She had to be satisfied with the knowledge that Miss Charity was doing her best under terrible circumstances. From what she said, England of the nineteenth century was teeming with poor people.

Still, Katie felt she had to do what she could to stop the kidnapping. Was Mother James on her way to abduct the boys now? No, likely she'd go back to Pod first. They didn't actually have an arrangement yet and she wouldn't do anything without the certainty of being paid.

Katie quickly excused herself and hustled Samantha out the door. "Why are you in such a hurry?" Samantha asked crossly. "We've searched for Nicholas for weeks. Now we've finally found him and you want to rush off again."

Katie explained her concern that children were in immediate danger. "You're probably right," Samantha agreed. "All right, let's hurry to Pod's hideout."

They ran directly to their listening spot. Katie pressed her ear to the crack and heard Mother James say, "Oi've come t' talk 'bout snatching little uns. Can fetch 'em but needs time. There's a coupla lads wot comes t' park arternoons. Good 'n' strong, though smallish. Reckon lads 're worth good few bob."

"See that you git 'em 'ere in arternoon," said Pod. "We'll 'ide 'ere 'til yuz comes."

"Lads won' be in park t'day. Still 'oliday fer rich folk. Oi'll git 'em day arter," Mother James told him.

Pod quickly revised his demand. "Bring 'em t'morra then," he said.

The girls shrank in the shadows as they heard the door open and close, then the shuffle of Mother James's feet in the alley as she departed.

Before Katie and Samantha left the shack, they clearly heard Pod say, "No need t' pay fer lads. Us'll git 'em oursel'." His cruel laugh sent shivers down Katie's spine.

— Chapter 17 —
A Terrible Happening!

Safely back at Samantha's house, the girls stepped into the midst of a Victorian family Christmas. Samantha's parents were so engrossed in their books, they didn't even realize the girls had been gone. Mama looked up just long enough to tell them to get ready for the evening meal.

In Samantha's room, the girls washed their faces and hands at the big china bowl that Daisy had filled with warm water. As they changed into clean clothes for supper they talked in low, intense voices, trying to put together the information they'd gleaned from their afternoon of sleuthing.

"Mother James said they go to the park every afternoon," said Katie. "She also said that they're small but well-fed and strong. Samantha, don't you think it sounds like she's describing Siggi and Wilbur?"

Samantha gasped. "Oh my goodness! Do you really think she's talking about them?"

"Nicholas said the laws have been changed and tightened, but he also said that there were greedy mine-owners who still use black-market child labour," Katie continued, her voice squeaking with fear. "I really think Pod is planning to sell Siggi and Wilbur as mine workers, and that the boys are in danger. Samantha, we have to do something!"

Katie fretted through the evening meal, then got little sleep that night. The more she thought about it, the more she was sure she was right. By morning, she knew what she had to do. First she had to get Samantha's help. She laid out her plan to her friend as they dressed for the day.

Samantha asked at breakfast for her parents' permission to accompany Nanny and the little boys to the park that afternoon.

"Whatever your mother says," muttered Papa absentmindedly as he read the morning Times.

Samantha turned to her mother, "Please, Mama," she wheedled. "Since football is over for the season, Katie and I can help Nanny with the boys."

"Goodness knows she could use your help," said her mother. "Those children have too much energy!" She thought a moment, then continued. "But, I think not. If I know Nanny, she would feel responsible for you girls as well as the little boys. She has enough to do."

Samantha was shocked. Her mother usually gave in to her requests. But she could tell by her tone that this time it would be useless to continue begging.

"Nanny shouldn't take the boys to the park today," Katie blurted out in panic.

"Why ever not, dear?" asked Samantha's mother.

Samantha kicked her under the table and glared at her, so Katie bit her lip and didn't say any more.

"What do we do now?" Katie asked Samantha when they were out of earshot. Samantha had no reply. With mounting dread, they helped Nanny dress the boys in their winter-weight sailor suits, flat-brimmed hats, and warm navy jackets. "I like when Nanny dresses the boys fashionably," Samantha said. "It makes them look like they come from a respectable family. Which we are," she added, shaking her long hair back from her face.

Katie was shocked that Samantha could even think about such trivialities when her brother was in danger. She watched fearfully from the nursery window as Nanny proudly trundled the baby, bundled warmly in his pram, down the street to the park. The two boys followed behind, the ribbons on their hats fluttering in the warmest breeze they'd had in weeks. She had been desperately trying to think of a reason to keep the boys at home. She was certain they were in terrible danger but Samantha still refused to let her tell anyone.

"If you told, it would alert Mama and Papa to what we've been up to and they'd refuse to let us out, ever again," she hissed.

Katie figured it was better to go to the park and try to protect the boys than to waste time arguing at home, so she reluctantly agreed to Samantha's terms.

As she'd done so many times, Samantha made up a story to explain to her mother why she and Katie needed to go out. "You know how much Katie enjoys clothes, but they're so different in Canada. May I take her to the high street to see the latest fashions?" she asked sweetly. The desire to see the latest fashions was something her mother understood completely. "Yes, of course, dear. What a splendid idea." Of course Samantha had no intention of taking Katie window shopping.

Katie and Samantha rode their horses to the park. Because it was a pleasant day there were nursemaids with prams everywhere. Which way to turn? Then Katie spied two children wearing flat-brimmed, ribboned hats playing with little boats on runners at the frozen edge of the pond. She pointed. Samantha nodded. Sure enough, there was Nanny, sitting on a bench nearby, closely watching the boys as though she was afraid they'd venture out onto the dangerous ice. Her hand stayed on the pram's handle, which she rocked without taking her eyes off Siggi and Wilbur. Katie and Samantha knew there was greater danger at hand than any Nanny was prepared for.

Angled off from the walking path near Nanny's bench was a bridle path for horses and riders. The girls guided their mounts onto this path. They came to a small opening in some shrubbery where there were posts for securing horses so the riders could enjoy the park on foot. Katie and Samantha had just slipped from the backs of their horses when they heard children yelling from the direction of the pond. Then a woman's scream.

The girls quickly untied their horses, leaped onto them, and galloped back the way they had come. They arrived at Nanny's bench just in time to see Pod and Rats, mounted on two swift ponies, gallop headlong down the path, leaving Nanny weeping and shaking her fists at them. Clutched tightly in front of each ruffian was a small boy struggling to get free. Pod had Siggi, whose sailor hat had flown off in the struggle, and Rats had Wilbur, whose hat was also left behind.

Katie and Samantha gave chase. The villains' ponies were fast, but burdened by two riders each. The girls got close enough for Samantha to yell, "Hang on boys. We'll save you."

Katie was focused entirely on saving Siggi. Her former desire to get rid of him was long gone. She leaned forward, urging Peggy to more speed.

She called out to Siggi, "Grab my hand!" Siggie yelled back, "Katie!" and reached out his little arm toward her. Just before their fingers touched, Peggy left the ground.

"Katie!" Siggi screamed in terror.

Katie pulled on the reins and yelled, but Peggy seemed not to notice. The little horse flew on. Katie was beside herself. She desperately wanted to go back, but she had no idea how. After a while Peggy circled as she had before. When they touched earth, it was in the snow-covered field at Haggarty's Ranch.

Katie rode in the field for some time, trying to get Peggy to take to the air. Finally she abandoned hope and rode her pony back to the barn. She didn't blame the little horse for coming home at the worst possible moment. She sensed that the pony had no more control over these strange flights than she had. She gave Peggy a rubdown, fed and watered her, and made sure she was comfortable in her stall before she headed home.

Katie was in a terrible state. She was full of guilt for putting Siggi in such danger. She was sure that Pod would sell him into a kind of slavery in the mines. How would Siggi be treated? Would he be fed enough? Would he be beaten? He was so little, so helpless. She had to get back to help him.

And Katie was afraid for herself, too. She had to face her parents. They had trusted her with Siggi's care and she had failed. At one time, she had wanted him to disappear, but that seemed like a long time ago.

How could she tell her parents that she had lost Siggi? And how could she even begin to tell them that she'd lost him in another country in another time?

Katie burst through the door. Mom and Dad were still at the table with their newspapers, mugs of coffee in front of them, just as when she'd left. They looked at their daughter and were shocked. Katie's face was swollen, her eyes red from crying.

Mom was at her side, gathering her in her arms, her face full of concern.

"Mom, Dad, sit down," Katie said. "I have to tell you something important, something you're not going to believe, but it's true. Peggy can fly." She watched her parents' faces. Dad looked incredulous. Mom had an unusual look. She was listening intently. Katie continued. "Not only can she fly to other places, but, even more strange, to a different time. She's taken me to England, but not the England of our time, to the England of the 1890s! I've met Samantha, the girl in my book. She's real!"

Katie had to stop for a moment to catch her breath. Her parents were silent. "Now I've got something really terrible to tell you." She gulped. "The last time I went back in time, I accidentally took Siggi with me. Now I'm here and he's there, all alone, and I think he's in awful danger and it's all my fault." Tears welled in her eyes.

When she saw the devastated look on her parents' faces, Katie felt even worse. Her mother gasped, "Siggi! My God! We have to get him back! He can't look after himself. He's just a little boy."

Then Mom gathered herself. She started to speak. She also had a strange story to tell. She would often pause in her telling of it and turn to Dad for confirmation or for further explanation. Sometimes the words tumbled out of both her parents at the same time, making their story incomprehensible. Then they had to tell that part again so Katie could understand. Katie's eyes widened with amazement. Their story was as incredible as hers. But she had no trouble believing every word.

They told her that when they were about Katie's age they had time-travelled too, several times. They later realized that they had gone to the past when they had been feeling unhappy with their lives. Their experiences in the past taught them that all families have challenges, many much greater than theirs. They told her the time-travel stopped once they had learned how to be happy in their own homes.

Mom explained, "I was so unhappy at your age, Katie. As you know, my parents died when I was very young so I was raised by my Great Aunt Kate. She did the best she could but she wasn't loving. On my first trip back in time, and the next, I was part of wonderful families who gave me the love I needed. On my third and final trip to the past, I met the young Aunt Kate and finally came to understand her. I discovered that she had always loved me, more than I thought."

She got choked up, so Dad stepped in. "I always had loving parents but I couldn't adjust after my accident and amputation. I was about your age when I lost my legs. My experiences in the past helped me mature. It's because of those experiences that I now have a full life."

Katie hugged her dad; then, from his arms, she looked at her mother. Mom's eyes were full of tears. "Oh, Katie," she said, "I'm sorry you felt so threatened by Siggi. But you see, when I travelled to the 1890s, I befriended a boy named Nicholas Camper. He came from an orphanage in London to a farm in Manitoba near the one where I was living."

"Nicholas Camper?" Katie spluttered, trying to process what her mother was saying. "I know a Nicholas Camper. I met him in London. Could it be that you and I know the same boy?"

Mom looked stunned, also trying to process this information. "Katie, you must have met him before he came to Canada." She paused, sorting out the pieces of the puzzle in her mind. "You'll be interested in this. I learned what happened to Nicholas after I came back to my own time. When he grew up he married another friend of mine, an immigrant from Iceland named Kristjana. I had grown close to both of them in 1890s Manitoba. Siggi is their great-great grandson." Katie's jaw dropped. "So that's why we felt we had to take Siggi into our family when his mother died," Mom continued. "Now you can see why I wasn't able to explain why he was so important to me. How could we expect you to believe such an unbelievable story?"

Katie was taking a long time to absorb everything. "I thought Nicholas looked familiar, somehow, but I couldn't figure it out," she said. "I saw his photograph in the album from Siggi's mother."

Mom rambled on, trying to cram everything in, as if a dam had burst. She took Katie onto her knee. "We haven't talked about our time-travelling with anyone except my Aunt Kate before she died. You're named after her—Aunt Kate and my childhood friend, Colleen. You're named after them both, my own little Katie Coll." Tears spilled from her eyes, and her hand shook a little as she stroked Katie's hair.

"When I researched what had happened to Nicholas after I came back to my own time, it was an easy matter to find his descendants. Siggi's mother knew me as a friend of the family. She never knew the whole story. But she knew me well enough to trust me with her child. I was honoured that she felt that way, but it wasn't for her sake alone that I wanted to give Siggi a home. I felt compelled to help Siggi because of my friendship with his great-great grandparents.

"Although we're trying hard to make little Siggi part of our family," Mom continued, "I want you to know that your father and I don't love you any less than we always have." She cradled Katie's face in her hands. "Katie, my child, love isn't something so small that someone can steal away your share. It's big, endless, and it can stretch to include more and more people. Your dad and I felt that the love in our family could stretch to include Siggi. We hoped you would feel the same."

"Instead, I acted horrid."

"You said it," said Dad, taking the sting out of his words by grinning. He took both Mom and Katie in his arms. Tears were in his eyes, too.

Katie was sure now that both Mom and Dad understood her pain and confusion and guilt. Maybe they had understood her all along, but she hadn't wanted to see it.

Once the three of them had recovered their composure, they had some serious thinking to do. How on earth could they get Siggi safely home?

The only thing Katie could think to do was to ride Peggy as much as possible in the hope that she would fly back to Victorian England. Mom and Dad didn't really want Katie to time-travel again, but they knew from their own experience that she would return and that time would stand still while she was gone. They all wanted Siggi safe, and, as Katie pointed out, Peggy was his only way home. "If I didn't do something to bring him back, I'd never forgive myself for wishing he would disappear from our lives," she said.

It turned out that none of them had any control over events. Katie was exercising Peggy a few days later when she suddenly realized it was happening again. But this time there was a difference. Peggy hit the ground in the park at a dead gallop. This time they were picking up precisely where they had left off. The girls on their horses were gaining ground on Pod and Rats—at least they were, until Jimbo stumbled and threw Samantha in the middle of the path. Katie had to pull up to prevent her pony from trampling her friend. Peggy reared, and before she knew what was happening, Katie was on the ground, too.

—Chapter 18—
Disaster

"Are you all right?" Katie asked as she scrambled to her feet.

"I think so," Samantha answered hesitantly, carefully checking to make sure no bones were broken. "Are you all right?" she asked, laughing. She was actually enjoying all this.

"Katie!" yelled Siggi. Katie whirled around to see Pod, still clutching Siggi, pull up and grab Peggy's reins. "No!" she screamed. At first, the pony resisted as Pod tried to lead her away. Katie knew she was no match for Pod's strength; she'd never be able to wrestle the reins out of his grasp. Seeing her chance, she ran and clambered onto the saddle and held on to the post tightly as Pod took off with the pony following behind. Katie laughed from her perch. If Pod was going to steal Peggy, he'd get her, too! Rats was waiting at the side of the path on his pony, riding bareback with Wilbur in front of him. Pod looked back at Katie, his face full of venom. "Git off roit quick if you know wot's good fer y'. Y'll slow us down," he shouted.

"Good!" she shouted back. She refused to dismount. She would go wherever Siggi and Peggy went and she would save them both—somehow.

Katie had managed to pull herself upright on her saddle. Pod let Peggy's reins go slack momentarily as he pulled up alongside Rats. With slight movements of her legs and body, Katie was able to position Peggy between her captors' ponies.

"Stop! Police!"

Katie turned to see two policemen followed by Nanny pushing the pram, all running toward them. Rats jumped and Pod's head whipped round. In that split second, Katie reached out and grabbed both Siggi and Wilbur by their jackets.

"Wilbur!" Nanny yelled. The little boy twisted with all his might. Rats lost his grip, and Wilbur, with Katie still holding tight to his jacket, fell to the ground, bringing Katie with him. She lost her grip on Siggi's jacket.

"Siggi! Peggy!" she screamed, scrambling back to her feet. But it was too late.

"'Ere!" Pod thrust Peggy's reins into Rats's now empty fist. They were off, Pod still clutching Siggi, Peggy following Rats, leaving Katie and everyone else in their dust.

As the ponies galloped through the park gates, Mother James was entering. She staggered back from the horses. She shook her fist at Pod and Rats. "Y' rotten li'l boogers. Th' lad's roitly mine. Oi coulda got good brass fer 'im. Ya promised." She took off after the thieves, her arms pumping, her black stockings showing as her skirts flew up.

Katie could hear Siggi yelling, "Help, help!" as he disappeared around a bend in the path. It broke her heart, but unlike Mother James, she knew there was no use following on foot. Where were Samantha and Jimbo?

As if in answer, her friend pulled up on her black horse. The policemen were busy trying to interrogate Nanny who was holding Wilbur in her arms, crying with relief.

"Samantha, please can I have Jimbo? I need to follow Pod," said Katie.

"If you're going, I am, too."

"What about your brother?"

"Nanny will look after him. Let's go!"

Katie clambered onto Jimbo's back behind Samantha.

"Come on!" Katie yelled, holding tight. "They've got a head start!"

Katie was frantic. Pod, Siggi, Rats, and Mother James had all disappeared by the time the girls rode Jimbo out of the park. They agreed to go directly to the hideout; it was the only place they knew to look for the thieves.

Katie felt sick about the whole situation. She had been so unfair to little Siggi. She had blamed him for her unhappiness, but now she was sure he had been innocent all along. He was just a hurt little kid missing his mother. He had needed a big sister to be kind to him, but she had just blamed him for everything going wrong in her own life. Because of her, he was separated from his new family just when he was starting to trust Mom and Dad. She knew the only way she could relieve her awful sense of guilt was to rescue him and take him back home.

Samantha once again left Jimbo at a hitching post and the girls headed for Pod's shack. They entered the familiar alleyway, ducking quickly into the shadows. Pod came out of the shack, dragging Siggi with him. He was dressed much like Pod's gang members now, in ragged clothes with only an old jacket to keep him warm. Pod likely intends to sell his good clothes, Katie thought.

Pod mounted Peggy and positioned the boy in front of him, then took the lead ropes of the pair of stolen ponies that had been tied outside. He must have come back to drop off Rats. As Peggy trotted off down the alley, the ponies behind, Pod shouted back, "Ya stop inside, Rats, 'til Oi tell ya differen'. Oi've got work t' do." Katie and Samantha followed him surreptitiously.

Siggi had stopped struggling. He seemed to have given up. Katie couldn't take her eyes off his slack little figure. How could she rescue both him and Peggy?

In the heavy traffic of the high street Peggy slowed to a walk, so the girls found it easier to keep up. They walked and walked, Katie's mind in a whirl. Finally Samantha stopped stock-still and refused to budge.

"I can't go a step farther! My feet are aching."

"You go home then," Katie snapped. Her feet were aching, too. "Make up a story to explain why I'm not with you. You're usually able to pull the wool over your parents' eyes."

"For your protection," Samantha shot back. "Every time I tell my parents a falsehood, it's because of you or your brother!"

"Not true! You don't care what you tell them as long as you get your own way." Katie walked away. She had no time to argue. Peggy was now more than two blocks ahead of them.

She began jogging to catch up, waving good-bye to Samantha without turning to look at her. She didn't feel good leaving her friend on a sour note, but she couldn't risk losing sight of Peggy and Siggi. At this point all she wanted was for her family to be together again, with Peggy safe in Haggarty's barn.

—Chapter 19—
Katie on Her Own

Finally Pod turned Peggy off the high street. Katie's nose told her they were near the docks. The familiar stench of decay and filth was now sharpened with the odour of rotting fish and seaweed. Pod rode along a rundown street full of wagons and carts overflowing with goods. The noise was terrible. Snorts, bawls, and neighs mixed with the creaking of wheels and shouts of drivers swinging their whips at all who blocked their way, humans as well as beasts. Katie plodded along with other pedestrians who had no choice but to take the middle of the road where they were sprayed by cold slush from passing vehicles. Katie's stomach turned as her nose was assaulted by the reek of manure, rotting seaweed, and fish, mixed with damp, decaying wood.

Pod rode directly to the door of an old, dilapidated building. The sign above the doorway read Strongman and Sons Shipping.

Katie watched as Pod gave Peggy's reins and the other ponies' leads to a boy who must have worked for the shipping company. Then Pod half-carried the squirming Siggi inside the building, behind a poor, ragged man pulling a skeleton of a girl along by the hand.

Katie knew she couldn't approach Peggy. The ponies were being watched by the boy who had led her to a watering trough. So she huddled in the shade of the building near the partially open door. First she heard a wavering pleading voice, then a man answering in something like a growl. "No' chance. If I wuz to take the gul, inspectors'd be all o'er us like ants on 'oney jar. The law says no lads under twelve an' no lasses 't all."

"But y' tike lads under twelve," pleaded the poor man. "I know some who got good piece a brass for their little uns. An' this 'ere gul's strong as lad. Please, good sir. We can't feed all our little uns. We've five, an' she's the only one big enough t' work."

"I 'ave to take m' chances with young lads. Mine-owners need little fellas wif little fingers so they pays good brass fer 'em. Lasses ain't worth the trouble. Now take 'er and be gone or I'll send yuz bof t' workhouse."

With that the poor man left the building with his daughter, grim-faced, brushing past Katie without looking at her.

Katie digested what she had just heard. She had been right all along. Siggi had been snatched because little boys were needed to work in the mines, no matter what the law said. They were worth money and Pod knew it.

Katie could hear Pod's voice inside, but she couldn't make out what he was saying. After a moment of silence a young man came out the door. He didn't pay any more attention to Katie than the poor man had. He walked over to Peggy and the other ponies. He felt their legs, checked their hooves, then pried open their mouths to examine their teeth. Then he went back inside the building.

He closed the door so Katie couldn't hear anything. She had just left the doorway when Pod came out, slapping his cap on his head. She turned her back so he wouldn't see her face. She sneaked a peek at him as he walked off down the street, whistling happily. Katie was sure she knew what that bulge in his back pocket was. He had just completed a very successful business deal. He had sold Siggi plus three ponies, including Peggy. The Icelandic pony and the little boy were to work in the dark of the coal mines.

Katie knew what she had to do. If girls couldn't work in the mines, she'd have to impersonate a younger boy. She was twelve, but small for her age. She was sure she could do it. The first thing was to find the right clothes.

Time was of the essence if she wanted to sail north on the same ship as Peggy and Siggi. Otherwise, she'd never be able to find them. She was scared of what lay ahead, but she had to do this.

Another poor family walked to the office doorway of Strongman and Sons. The father was carrying a well-worn bag with frayed carrying handles. Katie could see clothing protruding from the open top of the bag. With the man was an old woman who could barely put one foot in front of the other, and two ragged boys.

"Look out below." The shout came from a window above the office. Katie and the man both looked up and saw someone ready to empty a chamber pot into the street. The man quickly put down the bag so he could pull the woman out of the way. The boys huddled close to them, looking up, and no one noticed as Katie grabbed the bag and dashed behind the building.

She made sure no one was watching, then rifled through the bag. She found a pair of boy's pants, a shirt, a cap, and a ragged jacket. She pulled off her riding outfit with its heavy wool jacket and put on the shirt, making sure her locket was well-hidden. Next, the trousers, which were a bit too big. Then the jacket. Unfortunately, there were no boots. Her own pointed-toe riding boots would be a give-away. Her stockings would be okay without boots. The part that showed below the trousers looked like socks. Once they got wet, they wouldn't be good for warmth, but they'd at least hide her soft, uncalloused feet. She realized, however, that these stockings, too, would give her away. They were too clean, too good.

Rifling farther, at the bottom of the bag, she found a box. She feared that this poor family had put everything of any value in this bag when they left their home, but she was desperate. In the box were an old wedding ring, a knife, and a piece of rope. The knife was sharp so she easily chopped off her long hair, stuffing the strands in the dead weeds along the back of the building. The cap covered the spiky ends of her hair. The trousers kept sliding down, so she threaded the piece of rope through the belt loops and tied it around her waist. Next she rubbed her feet in the dirt until her stockings looked as if she'd walked in them for miles. To make them look more worn, she poked holes in them with the knife, one hole letting a toe show, another baring a heel. Finally, she took a bit of dirt in her hand and dabbed her nose and chin, wiping both off so only streaks remained. Now she looked like a poor boy, she hoped.

Thinking of the family she'd stolen from, she put her discarded boots and riding outfit in the bottom of the bag, hoping someone would find them useful. Perhaps they could be sold. Then she put the knife back in the box beside the ring and set it back in its place under the clothes.

She returned to the street and put the bag down just as the unsuspecting owners came out of the office, without the boys. The old woman was crying. The man looked angry. He glanced at the bag with some surprise as if he'd forgotten about it, then picked it up. He looked directly at Katie without a hint of curiosity, took the woman's arm, and walked slowly away, the bag dangling from his arm.

Katie wished she could see herself in a mirror, but the man's lack of reaction gave her confidence in her disguise. Now she had to concoct a story and be ready for the next part of her plan.

Taking a deep breath, she walked into the office.

A tall, stooped man seemed to hover over the counter. "Come in, boy," he said in a high-pitched, wheedling kind of voice. "Wot can I do fer ye?"

"Me nime's Stevie," said Katie, trying to sound like Pod. "Oi've run from 'ome an' Oi needs work."

"You mean you don' 'ave parents close by?" said the man.

"I won' go 'ome," she said, stomping her foot on the floor for emphasis. "I won' stop in school one more day!"

"Well, well, well. Today's m' lucky day, and not a farthing to pay," he said under his breath. Then out loud he said, "I 'ave work fer ya. Go int' that back room, boy. We'll get ya when time comes t' board ship."

He didn't even ask my last name, thought Katie. I guess names aren't important to slave-traders.

The back room smelled like sweat and dirty clothes. It took a few minutes for her eyes to adjust to the gloom. She scanned the room for Siggi but didn't spot him. The room was full of ragged boys, all dressed much like she was. She saw the two young lads from the family who'd just left. She was sure they'd recognize their clothes, but they didn't pay any attention to her and she started to think her disguise must be working. It took another minute of desperately scanning the room before she spied Siggi, looking terrified as he huddled alone in a corner. It was all she could do not to rush to console him, but she didn't dare. He might call out her name and expose her as the fraud she was. She saw him glance her way, his eyes flicking past, but then he quickly looked back at her. She must look familiar. She ducked her head and hoped he wouldn't say anything to give her away.

After a few minutes the tall stooped man came in and shooed

them out a back door. "Jist do wot carman sez, 'ear?" Waiting for them in the back alley was a rough-looking fat man carrying a whip and sitting on a wagon pulled by a team of horses. "Git in," he snarled at the children. Before they started off, the boy who had examined Peggy tied her and four other ponies to the back of the wagon box. All must have passed inspection.

The carman swore loudly at the team of horses and the wagon lurched off. Up the road they went, then down a narrower one, the smells getting stronger and the noises louder as they progressed. They stopped when the carman guided the team into a long line of horses and wagons at a wharf. Theirs was the only vehicle loaded with people instead of goods. Katie's feet were half-frozen.

Katie heard the dockworkers say the ship was going to Newcastle-upon-Tyne. She remembered Samantha's father saying that Newcastle was north of London and that there were big coal mines there. She saw Siggi staring at her, and when she thought they weren't being watched, she shook her head. She wasn't sure if he could see through her disguise, but she didn't want anyone to find out she was an imposter. There was a ship at the wharf. Dozens of workers were unloading goods from wagons, packing them into barrows, and wheeling them up a ramp to the deck. Katie almost called out to Peggy when a dockworker led the ponies onto the ship, but she bit her tongue.

A worker shouted at the boys, "Lads, climb down from wagon, sharpish now, and git on boa'. Sailor 'll show yez wer ladder goes down b'low."

The children followed his instructions and when they reached a dark room down below, they sat on the floor or leaned against the walls, and waited. It was so dark Katie couldn't see anyone's face.

She had no idea where Siggi was in the darkness.

The ship set sail. The dirty old boat creaked and groaned as it listed this way and that. Some of the boys were seasick. The smell was awful. Then Katie heard a boy crying. It made her feel like weeping, too.

She just wanted to get out of this horrid place. But she'd heard the key turn in the lock and knew they were prisoners. A long time passed during which she drifted in and out of sleep. Because of the darkness, she had no idea if it was day or night. Katie felt weak from hunger and her stomach ached, but there was no sign of food for the children. Finally the ship docked, and the door was unlocked. Katie and the others stumbled to the ladder and climbed wearily up to the deck. She sucked in a great lungful of cold, damp winter air. Compared to the putrid air below decks, this seemed fresh and clean.

The journey from the docks of Newcastle to the mine was much like the journey to the docks in London. A wagon to carry the boys, ponies trotting behind, a burly carman threatening both boys and horses with a whip. After a long ride through the teeming streets of a big city, then empty countryside, they came to a cluster of buildings and stopped. Some of the buildings were high, like towers, and some were low. There was a sign that said Diamond Collieries in huge, black letters over a low building. Workers bustled everywhere like ants. Katie saw two giant steam engines and a train track leading to a wide doorway.

She was hustled off the wagon with the other new boys, and they were all taken to the low building with the sign. They were so cold from the ride they were almost glad when they were herded into a stuffy room where there was a long, rough wood table. On the table someone had set mugs of milky tea and huge platters of bread spread with dripping, the cooled and hardened fat from roast meat. Although it was very greasy, Katie gobbled it down. It was the first food she'd eaten since she'd left Samantha's house. When her bread was gone and the mug was empty, she reached for more, but the carman, still carrying his whip, growled, "You've already 'ad yurs," so she stepped back.

The carman threw her a musty-smelling blanket and told her to find a spot to sleep. She found an empty place on the floor and lay down without speaking a word. The floor was hard but they were all exhausted. Soon the room was filled with snores. Katie fell asleep with her hand on her precious locket, and dreamed of taking Peggy and Siggi home.

Breakfast the next morning was a replica of the evening meal. Before they ate, the boys were all allowed to use the office toilet out back. Katie was surprised to find a flush toilet in the little shed, a remarkable contrast to the outdoor toilet her family had behind their cabin in the Yukon and the chamber pots in Samantha's house. The mine-owners must be very rich, she thought.

After breakfast, the new young workers were told to walk in twos to the entrance to the mines. Siggi found a little boy to walk beside. Katie still didn't know whether he recognized her; if he did, he was too scared to let on. She avoided the boys whose clothes she was wearing and walked with a lad about her size. His name was Harvey, or, as he said it, "'arvey." He limped, and when he saw her looking at his bowed legs he said, "Us 'ave th' rickets. Me bones gone soft."

Back in school in Thunder Bay, Katie had learned that if children didn't get proper food and enough sunshine, they might get this or other awful conditions. Her teacher had explained that few children in Canada were so undernourished, but that these ailments were still common in poor countries. When she first arrived at Samantha's house, Katie had the impression that England in the nineteenth century was a rich, modern country, the same as it was in her own time. Her book on Victorian England had told only about the middle class, like Samantha's family. Katie's experiences in the East End and now here at the mines gave her a different story.

She saw a vast gulf between poor people and those with enough money to live comfortably. Samantha's family had a warm home, good clothing, and more than enough food. But for so many others, like Nicholas, Mother James and her brood, and the boys trudging to the mine, life was just plain unfair. Katie was seeing real poverty for the first time in her life.

Katie knew from what her mother had told her that Nicholas had many hardships ahead of him in Canada, but that he would go on to a successful life. And Siggi was part of Nicholas's future—at least he would be if the little boy wasn't trapped in time. Both boys' happiness depended on her getting Siggi home. She knew it was up to her—and Peggy, of course.

—Chapter 20—
Coal Mining

The carman with the whip did a quick sorting of the new workers. "Smallish lads 'll be trappers. Stan' each b' each o'er 'ere. Any lads ever worked wif 'orses?"

Four of the boys, including Katie, put up their hands. It was all she could do not to jump up and down to make him notice her. The carman came over and felt her biceps. She scowled and shook his hand off her arm. "Smallish. No' strong," he said. "'E'll be driver." He picked the other three who'd held up their hands to be drivers, too. The bigger, stronger boys were told they'd be haulers. The new groups stayed together as they re-formed the line and each boy was given a can of water to drink during his shift. Katie walked with a different boy now—Harvey was with the trappers.

As the shivering, poorly dressed boys inched up to one of the tall, tower-like buildings, Katie could see inside. Grown men were at the front of the line. They were dressed alike in heavy work pants and boots with a jacket and vest over a dark shirt, and all wore cloth caps. Each carried a lantern, a pick and shovel, and a can of water.

A few men crowded into the small cage and the door clanged shut behind them. The cage was hitched to a moving cable that pulled it quickly down into a dark hole. In a matter of minutes the empty cage was back to take the next small group. The boys were approaching the front of the line, but they had to wait as the new ponies were brought through.

Peggy was first. Katie thought her pony would be led into the cage, but no. The cage was lifted high and leather slings hooked to its bottom were fastened around Peggy's body. She was lifted off her feet, head up and tail down, as the cage was lifted even higher. Katie could imagine how terrified Peggy would be, but she didn't dare speak. The little Icelandic pony neighed and struggled to free herself from the harness. But she must have sensed that struggle was hopeless, for after a while she kept her body completely still, except for an uncontrollable shuddering of hide over muscles, as she disappeared down the shaft. Katie could see the pony's eyes rolling, the whites flashing in terror.

"That's Smokey gone below," said a worker. "Now Pete and Flame." Katie made a mental note that Peggy was now Smokey.

After the last terrified pony was taken below, the cage, packed with tubs of coal now, came up to the top of the shaft. The tubs were unloaded. A group of women shovelled the coal from the tubs into carts lined up by the train tracks. "Women c'n still work above groun'," the boy behind Katie muttered to his partner.

When it was his turn, one of the boys refused to get in the cage; he was too scared. A worker pushed him in with the others, and they disappeared down into the dark. Katie thought of her little brother and of how scared he must be.

Now it was time for Katie and the other drivers to go down. The four of them were so thin, they were able to get into the empty cage together. Even though the cable attached to the cage was really thick, Katie was still scared that it might break. Once the door clanged shut, the cage plunged to the bottom of the shaft in seconds, making her feel as though had left her stomach at the top.

At first she couldn't see much in the dim lantern light, but soon her eyes adjusted. What she saw lifted her spirits. Peggy—or Smokey—was waiting in a long tunnel along with the other ponies. A man beckoned to Katie and the other drivers. "Oi's 'orse-keeper," he said, "and ya mus' do as Oi sez." He spoke directly to Katie. "This beas' is yers to ker fer." He pointed to a brown gelding. "Tis worth a nice piece o' brass, so ker fer it good or else you'll be sorry."

"I don' wan' tha' 'orse," Katie said firmly. The man grinned at her stubbornness, but his grin had an edge to it that frightened her. He pointed to Peggy and asked, "Duz Smokey suit yer?" She nodded, relieved that she hadn't made him angry. Not this time anyway.

The horse-keeper led the ponies and drivers on a seemingly endless walk, at least two miles, Katie reckoned, to where the miners were working. Water dripped down the walls around them. She felt a draft of fresh air and the man explained it came from a ventilation shaft that brought fresh air from the surface. "Miners used t' die from pizon air," he said. "Wif th' ventilators workin' t' bring air down 'ere we're safe now."

"Listen up," he continued, "and don' arsk questions." Katie had to learn to hitch Smokey to a coal tub, called a truck, that the pony would haul along rails to a loading spot where an underground train would pick them up. The trucks were already filled with coal. The boys working as haulers had pulled them to a bend in the track where they left the heavy trucks waiting for a pony to pull them the rest of the way. Once Smokey was trained to do her job without anyone leading her, Katie would be given some other ponies to care for as well.

Katie was shown where the ponies were housed underground, a stable with stalls and bins of corn, chopped hay, and grain stalks.

There were barrels of water against the wall so the drivers could water their ponies. The little horses wouldn't see the light of day for months; everything they needed was here. The stable was lit by dim electric lights strung along the walls.

"If there's fire or explosion, fetch ponies t' cage roit quick. They be tiken up firs'," said the horse-keeper. Katie wondered why. Surely they'd be just as concerned about getting people out as quickly as possible.

Katie worried about Siggi. Where was he? She hadn't said a word to him yet. If she could only talk to him without fear that he'd shout out her name or do something else to reveal she was not who she said she was.

In the first days of her new life, Peggy acted strangely lethargic. Katie felt the same way and put it down to the heat of the underground. One day she was complaining to a hauler who used to work as a driver. He said, "Yez'll be usta th' 'eat in week or two." Heaven forbid we'll be here that long, she thought.

The noise also exhausted her. It was so loud in the underground. The air was filled with the clatter of trucks running on the rails and the dull thuds of explosions to get at new seams of coal. Even the scurrying of rats was loud. In places the rails were on flat ground so the trucks hauling coal were easy to pull, but in other places, the grade was so steep Peggy had to hunker down and pull with all her might. Katie was most afraid of falling stones and chunks of coal breaking loose from overhead.

A couple of days after they started work, Flame's driver brought his pony back to the stable bleeding from a bad cut above her eye. The horse-keeper put healing ointment on it and bandaged it. Listening to the other miners, Katie had learned that the owners followed the laws for the pit ponies much more carefully than they did for human workers. She was shocked to discover that ponies were considered more valuable than people and figured it must be because they would bring more money. "If Oi'd been 'urt," Flame's driver whispered to her, "Oi'd not git such fas' 'elp."

After she groomed Peggy in the evenings, it was time for Katie and the other drivers to go up in the cage. Back on the surface, she felt a deep exhaustion and her feet needed bandaging. The footing in the mine was rough, so her feet kept getting cut. Her stockings were in such tatters and so blood-soaked that she finally threw them away.

The next morning the owners gave Katie a pair of boots and some new socks. "You'll need these to keep up with the work," they said.

Katie went down in the cage, feeling much better in her new boots. She had become adjusted to the heat of the underground; it didn't bother her as much as when she had started. As she hurried toward the stable, she saw someone hobbling along in front of her. She recognized the bowed legs.

"'Arvey! Wait up," she called as she ran to overtake him. He stopped and checked both ways in the tunnel to make sure they were alone before he answered.

"'Ello, Stevie. Wot?"

"'Ow are ya? They treatin' ya awroit?"

He looked at her in astonishment. "Mus' trap wi'out light. Wait for 'aulers to bring tubs o' coal, then mus' open trapdoors t' let 'em through. Oi opens the doors for th' air too. Air's pizon here so ya needs fresh. Lights go out alla' time. Oi allus wuz afeard o' dark. And the water comes up. Oi's afeard o' water. It's col'. When air is 'ot an' water's col', makes me legs swell. Soon I mut lose m' legs. Oi'm full o' fears."

As he spoke about possibly losing the use of his legs, Katie felt her throat closing and her mouth go dry.

"The little boy—trapper like you," she managed to croak, "is 'e doin' awroit?"

"Ya means Siggi? 'E tries 'ard but 'e's no' strong. 'E got beat by marster fer not openin' door right smart. 'Twas dun in front o' all to smarten us up. 'E's afeard too, since I told 'im 'e mut lose legs."

Katie was horrified. Siggi had been beaten! He must be frightened half to death. She had to get him out of here. Soon. That night she heard Siggi sobbing in his corner. In spite of her exhaustion, she lay awake long into the night. Try as she might, she couldn't see a way to rescue the little boy.

A few days later Katie was still trying to think of a way to save Siggi when she got lost. She took a wrong turn and went down a different tunnel. She didn't come to the stable when she should have. Confused, she turned another corner and suddenly, there he was.

Siggi was sitting, kind of hunched up, holding a piece of rope attached to a small but heavy-looking wooden door. Katie heard something rattling loudly and, as the noise got closer, Siggi hauled on the rope and the door opened. On the other side of it Katie could see a tub of coal making a terrible racket as a big boy pushed it along the track and through the door. Siggi had thrown most of his weight on the rope to hold the door open. The boy and the tub disappeared down the tunnel. Before the door swung shut, Katie saw a miner crouched down, working with a pick-axe at a coal seam by the pale light of a weak electric bulb. He was throwing chunks of coal into a tub.

Katie huddled near Siggi after the door was closed. He was coughing. Each cough caused his thin little body to heave and shudder. The air smelled bad here. "Siggi, I'm here," she said.

"Katie, is it really you?" he said, after he had caught his breath. "I thought I saw you a few times, but I wasn't sure it was you. Why are you dressed like a boy?" He started coughing and didn't speak again for a few minutes. "Katie, I'm sick and I want out of here. It's dark and I hear rats and sometimes the water comes up and I'm scared. I'm here for hours and there's no bathroom. I want to go up to the light and stay up!"

Katie was overwhelmed with relief to speak with the child. She wanted to get him out of this terrible place, right now, but knew she couldn't—not just yet.

"Siggi, hang in there," she told him. "They know me here as Stevie. Don't tell anyone my real name or that I'm a girl. I'll come to get you as soon as I can. Oh, Siggi," she was choking up, "I'm so glad I finally found you down here." She squeezed his shoulder as his little body convulsed with another fit of coughing. They heard another rattling and Siggi was barely able to get the door open before a huge tub of coal came hurtling through. Katie had to hug the wet wall to keep from being hit.

Reluctantly she left Siggi and found her way back to the stable and Peggy. She was sure she wouldn't be able to help her little brother—that's how she thought of him now—if she didn't keep her disguise, at least until she thought of a plan of action. She threw her arms around her pony's neck and sobbed, "Oh, Peggy. What am I going to do?".

Chapter 21

Accident

A few days later, Katie was leading Peggy and another heavy load of coal along the tracks, when she felt a tremor. Then came a terrible shaking, like an earthquake, and a big bang. She heard running feet and faraway shouts of "'old on, we'll get yuz out." The dim lights flickered and died. She was in total darkness.

Katie dropped Peggy's lead rope. "I have to find Siggi," she said to the little horse. Peggy was too valuable, she reasoned, for the mine-owners to risk her coming to harm, so it was okay to leave her. But it wouldn't matter to the callous owners if Siggi lived or died. There were many poor, desperate families willing to sell their children for a few coins to replace him. She knew she was his only hope.

She wanted to run but had to take care in the dark. She knew she should just retrace her steps from before but she wasn't sure where she was. She'd have to follow the sounds. She wasn't exactly sure what had happened. Had there been an explosion? She had heard about terrible explosions and fires in mines where dozens had died. She sniffed. The air was full of dust but she couldn't smell smoke. That was a relief, but if there had been a cave-in, people could be trapped or killed beneath fallen rubble. She'd heard that cave-ins were sometimes triggered by blasts to open more coal seams.

Someone was shouting far down the tunnel. She tripped on a rock and fell, hurting her leg. She got up and, with a hand on the side of the tunnel to guide her, she half-hopped, half-ran toward the sound. She could hear running toward her. She called out to them, "O'er 'ere! Oi'm Stevie, a driver."

A miner stopped. "Yer goin' wrong way, Stevie." Those with him ran on. "This lot's goin' t' cage," he said. "Come wi' us."

A big part of Katie wanted to go with this kind man. She hated to be so helpless in the dark, and she knew she might die if she didn't go with him. But she had to save Siggi, if she could. If she was afraid, she knew he'd be even more frightened. "Y' go afore," she said to the miner. "Oi'll foller." Then she kept going, listening to his footsteps gradually getting fainter behind her as he hurried to catch up with his mates.

After another few minutes, hoping to find the turn in the tunnel that led to Siggi, she stumbled against something big and hairy. She screamed, then pulled herself together. She forced herself to feel the object blocking her path. It didn't take long to figure out that it was the body of a pony, still warm but not moving or even twitching. Her hands found the mane and she stroked the neck, feeling more sad than horrified now. Near the head she felt a huge rock on the floor. She wished she knew which pony it was. But she couldn't stop to figure things out. She had to get to Siggi. And the only way was to climb over the dead pony's body.

Her stomach twisted and she felt like she was going to throw up. She crawled across the body, freeing herself every time a hand or foot got entangled in the pit harness. Thinking she was free, she tried to stand when her hand touched hair again. She felt around and realized this was another body. Not a pony this time, but likely the driver. Her hand was on his already cold face. She knew he wasn't breathing. There was nothing she could do for him. She shuddered, but she wouldn't let herself think of the dead boy. Not now. She didn't have time.

She stood up and, with a hand on the wall to guide her in the dark, she continued down the tunnel with a renewed sense of urgency.

As she strode along, her foot hit something hard, bringing her to a sudden halt. She stretched out her hands in the darkness and felt a barrier made of rocks and timbers. Then her ears picked up a muffled sound. She listened carefully. It was the sound of a child crying and coughing. Could it be?

"Siggi!" she shouted. "Is that you?"

"Stevie!" came a faint voice from the other side of the barrier. "Help me!"

"Oi'm comin'," she shouted back. She knew that Siggi called her Stevie for a reason. He wasn't alone. She wasn't sure if this was good or bad—it depended on who was with him. She started clawing at the caved-in rocks and timbers with her bare hands.

Every little while she called out to Siggi, "Oi'm comin'. Don' be afeared." Slowly a pile of rocks built up beside her as she worked, but the darkness slowed her down. Whenever she stopped, she heard noises from the other side; someone there was also working at clearing the passage. It seemed like hours passed. Her hands were scraped and hurting. When she put a banged knuckle in her mouth she tasted salty blood. Finally, there was a glimmer of light in front of her. A hole!

Through the hole she could see Siggi in the light of a lantern. A miner was clearing away the debris with a pick and shovel.

"Ta, laddy," he said to Katie when they met in the opening. "I bin workin' since the bump but no' gettin' far. I canna manage wi'out ya. M' frien's calls me Jimmy."

"Oi'm Stevie," said Katie, reaching through the hole to shake his hand.

When the hole was big enough, Katie reached for Siggi's hand and helped him over the rubble. Katie and Jimmy worked at making the hole bigger so Jimmy could climb through, too. He led them down the tunnel holding his lantern high.

A turn brought them to where the empty tubs were hauled back to be filled with coal again. Nearby stood a pony, alone. Could it possibly be hers? Yes, it was Peggy, still harnessed to a coal tub, standing patiently as though expecting someone.

"Oh! You waited for me!" Katie said, her voice full of emotion. She threw her arms around Peggy's neck. Then she freed Peggy from her harness.

"Listen lad," said Jimmy. "We're close to th' cage. Keep goin'."

"No' wi'out Smokey," Katie answered.

She helped Siggi, who was weak from coughing, onto Peggy's back, and led the pony the last mile or so.

When they reached the cage, it was bringing down rescuers from a nearby mine, all with lanterns and picks. They were delighted to find three survivors, all unhurt, and a pony that had survived, too. They immediately set to work fastening Peggy to the bottom of the cage, and she was hauled up to the surface.

Katie, Siggi, and Jimmy waited patiently for the cage to come back for them. Katie's hand went to her throat, under her shirt, feeling for the locket. It was gone! It must have come loose when she fell in the mine, or when she climbed over the pony. She'd never find it now. Although she felt terrible over its loss, she felt better knowing that she'd lost her precious locket while searching for Siggi, and now she'd found him. That was the important thing.

Safely on the surface, Jimmy was surrounded by his joyful family, all pulling at his clothes and crying and laughing at the same time. Katie saw other women and children whose exhausted, drawn faces reminded her of the men still trapped, or perhaps dead, below. But she couldn't think of that, not until she had gotten Siggi away from this terrible place.

With everyone's attention on getting more rescuers into the cage, Katie mounted Peggy with Siggi at her back. The lead rope would have to do to guide her pony. "We're going to the docks to catch the next boat to London, Siggi," she said to the sick little boy. He didn't say anything; anytime he tried to speak, he was overcome with a coughing spell. But she knew he must feel as relieved as she did to be in the fresh air, away from the horrors of the mine.

Katie was shaken and upset, but she pushed the memory of the dead pony and driver to the back of her mind. Once she and Siggi were safe at Samantha's house she could fall apart, but not yet.

Katie turned Peggy toward the gate, and urged her to a trot, feeling safer and safer the farther they went from that hated mine. She stopped at the mine office and dismounted, leaving Siggi with Peggy. The office was empty. All the office workers must be at the pithead waiting to see how many miners had been lost in the explosion. Katie went to the cash box, which was left unguarded in all the excitement. There was an open ledger beside it, listing the payments to the miners.

Katie looked in the ledger and made a quick calculation of what she and Siggi were owed for the weeks they had worked. She was surprised at how little it was. She took this amount and stuffed it into her pocket. She hoped this was enough to buy passage for the three of them. She thought that as long as she could afford passage for Peggy and Siggi, she, as Stevie, could work to pay her own way—she'd heard of people doing that. She wouldn't take more than the two of them had earned. She closed the box firmly and rushed back to Peggy and Siggi.

At the docks she found she had just enough money to buy passage for all three of them on a ship to London. Peggy was taken below with other horses, but this time Katie and Siggi stayed on deck.

It was getting dark when Katie, Siggi, and Peggy got to Samantha's house. Samantha was in the stable, just back from a ride on Jimbo. She stared at the strange boy standing in the doorway holding a very dirty child's hand. Katie explained as best she could. Samantha kept staring, for out of the mouth of this bedraggled boy was coming the voice of Katie. Finally the explanations sank in and Samantha was overjoyed to have her friend safely back.

"I've missed you so much," she squealed, hugging Katie. "But how did you get him?" she pointed at Siggi.

"I'm glad to be back, too," said Katie. "I'll tell you all about it later." Samantha hadn't said a word directly to Siggi, but when he coughed and coughed, she led the pair of them to the kitchen and told Daisy to take care of the little boy. Daisy called Nanny and when Nanny heard that Siggi was back, she rushed to the kitchen, gathered him in her arms and carried him upstairs to a hot bath and some soup—her remedy for all ills.

After a couple of bowls of soup and a long hot bath, Katie snuggled into her clean, comfortable bed. She knew Siggi and Peggy were both well-fed and safe. She thought of the horrors she had seen and suspected she would have bad dreams, but for now she felt safe and almost happy. She was truly glad to be back at her friend's house. Samantha was thoughtless and spoiled sometimes, but she didn't hold a grudge. It seemed she had forgotten her argument with Katie. Or perhaps she was so shallow, nothing mattered much to her.

Thoughtless and spoiled. Isn't that how Katie's dad had once described her? It had been true once, she knew, but was it still an accurate description? She had barely begun to ponder this when she fell into the deep sleep of exhaustion.

Chapter 22

A Family

First thing in the morning, Katie asked about Nicholas. "He went to Miss Charity's orphanage," Samantha told her. "So did Mother James's children." Katie was glad that Nicholas and the children were getting good care.

"Could we see him?" Katie asked.

"Of course," Samantha answered, "but first we must do something about your hair." Samantha gave Katie one of her hats to wear so no one would see her hacked-off hair, and that afternoon, the two of them rode up to a gigantic brick building that looked like a prison. A young boy appeared on the front lawn, beside the carriage path, suddenly and silently, like a ghost. "Oi'll look after your 'orses," he said.

In the big echoing entrance hall was a sign that almost covered the wall. "God Protect Our Orphans" was written on it in colourful scrolled letters. A housekeeper in a blue dress with a white apron and cap appeared as silently as the boy outside and asked the girls who they had come to see. Before Katie could answer, Miss Charity came through the door. She recognized the girls immediately and invited them to come into her office for tea.

Katie and Samantha sat in her spacious office, sipping their tea, listening to Miss Charity tell them how well Mother James's children were doing. "They have you to thank for that, Katie." Looking around the room, Katie noticed rows and rows of photographs covering the walls. Miss Charity followed her gaze. "Those are Lost Lambs' benefactors," she said.

"They must be very rich," said Samantha.

"Very rich, indeed," agreed Miss Charity. "The most respectable men of our city. You girls must excuse me. I have an appointment with one of our benefactors in about five minutes."

In answer to a bell hidden discreetly under Miss Charity's desk, a young female servant came in to clear away the tea things. Another appeared almost at once to give them a tour of the orphanage. The schoolrooms and the training rooms were in use so they went to the second floor and she showed them where the girls slept. In each of four huge dormitories there were row upon row of narrow metal beds placed tightly together. The white coverlet on each was spotless and pulled tight. Like in the army, Katie thought, remembering something Dad had once told her. Next they saw the library with shelves sparsely lined with books, a bathing room with rows of tin bathtubs hanging on the wall, a hospital room that smelled strongly of disinfectant, and a gymnasium, not in use at the moment.

"Oi'm in trainin' fer service," the little servant told them proudly. "Miss Charity sez Oi'm lucky, fer service is above m' station. Oi loiks it 'ere. Oi gits lotsa bread 'n' drippin' fer m' tea."

Just then, who should they run into but Nicholas, coming down the hall carrying a pair of old boots, their soles flapping. Katie was delighted to see him, and he looked happy to see them, too, but he peered anxiously over his shoulder before speaking.

"Marster mut 'ear," he said in a low voice. "Oi's spos'd t' be in bootmiking class." The little maid showed them into an empty room and left them there to talk.

Alone in the room with his friends, Nicholas was his old self. When he found out that Katie had rescued Peggy and Siggi from the mines, he was very excited. "Oi didn' know you 'ad li'l brother, Kitie," he said. "Yes, I do," she answered simply. Katie saw now that, except for their colouring, Siggi and Nicholas looked much alike.

"Oi'd loik 'ole story but don' 'ave toime now," he said.

"Do you like it here?" Katie asked.

"Don' min' it," he said. "M' belly's full, 'n' Oi'm learnin' m' da's trade. Lotsa boys don' loik it. Too many rules 'n' they sez food's better on stree'. Some boys wen' 'ta Canada day afore yistid'y. Each week some goes." Then his face fell and he looked very sad. "I miss me mum somethin' turrible. 'Er's gettin' be'er bu' 'er still too sick t' sew, so Oi can't go 'ome."

Nicholas excused himself and hurried off to class. Out in the hall, the girls spotted the little maid. They asked to see Mother James's children. The child took the girls to several classrooms where, as they peeked in, she pointed out different children from Mother James's brood. They all looked very clean and reasonably healthy.

As the girls rode home after their visit, Samantha chattered away about what a great place the orphanage was, but Katie wasn't so sure. If Mother James was wrong to kidnap innocent children, wasn't Miss Charity doing something similar by taking children from their parents? Yet, she thought she was saving them. Katie tried to puzzle it out. She hoped she would go home to the Yukon soon, but she'd like to talk longer to Nicholas so she could figure out how she really felt about Miss Charity and her orphanage. She wanted Mom's opinion, too, once she got home.

Both Siggi and Katie were glad to be at Samantha's house for the time being, but Katie kept hoping Peggy would take them back to their real home, in their real time, soon. Siggi was getting stronger each day. With good food and enough rest his cough was quickly disappearing and his strength was returning. At first he had terrifying nightmares, but Katie comforted him when she heard crying in the nursery. Nanny watched over him, too, but she said she understood that Siggi got more comfort from his sister than he did from her. Gradually, the nightmares stopped. Siggi became more thoughtful, quieter than he had been before he was kidnapped. He talked sometimes about his mother when he and Katie were alone, but his grief was becoming muted. "You're my bestest sister," he told Katie one day, in his old, exuberant way. He said he wanted to go home now, too. Home to Mom and Dad.

Katie felt different, too. Her struggles to save Siggi had shaken her to the core. After her first night back, she had many nights of frightening dreams about stumbling across dead ponies and drivers. She would wake crying, shaking, and soaked with sweat. But gradually, as the days passed, her spirits rose.

The biggest change in Katie was her feelings about Siggi. She fully understood now that what Mom had told her was true. Love isn't something that people can steal from you. If it's real, it can stretch to include more and more people.

As Katie changed, her feelings for Samantha changed. She didn't feel as close to Samantha now. Katie increasingly had little patience for Samantha's self-centred attitude, her snobbery, and her willingness to stretch the truth to get what she wanted.

Katie found herself thinking more and more of Mad. She would try harder to make friends when she got home. Looking back, she realized that Mad had no objection to Siggi. Katie was the one who had created a problem that wasn't there. I know I can speak up against bigotry, she thought, just like Mom and Dad taught me. I stood up for Siggi, and now I'm strong enough to stand up for Mad, too. Perhaps she and Mad would be close enough one day that she could tell her about her travels to the past.

Katie had also come to see that Samantha's parents were caricatures of good parents, not real and warm like her own parents. She was more anxious than ever to get home.

Katie knew she had no control over Peggy's flying, but she wanted to be prepared when the time came. In order to prevent a repeat performance of going home without Siggi, she insisted he ride with her each day after breakfast. Nanny took a bit of convincing, but she did admit that Siggi was growing up and getting more responsible, so she allowed him his daily ride, sitting safely behind his big sister. Katie didn't use a sidesaddle when Siggi was with her. Billy agreed to that change, but he still thought it scandalous for them to ride bareback. "Young Miss should use reg'lar saddle and wear proper clothes," he said. So she wore a split skirt, which still looked modest enough for Billy's and Nanny's approval.

It was on one of these rides, a short time later, that Peggy took to the air. Katie and Siggi both laughed with excitement and happiness. But instead of the long trip to the Yukon, as they had expected, quite soon the little horse circled and slowed but didn't land. Instead she hovered, close enough to the ground that Katie could see and faintly hear people below. She could tell by the people's dress and accents that she and Siggi were still in nineteenth-century England. They had a bird's-eye view of a dock, beside a big ship. A sign told them the docks were in Portsmouth.

Looking down at the passengers lining up to get on the ship, she understood why they had been brought here. There was Nicholas saying good-bye to his mother, and behind them was Miss Charity, shooing along a long line of children, including Mother James's brood. They were dressed in plain but sturdy clothes given by the orphanage. Siggi looked a little puzzled at the long lines of people getting on the ship.

"What's happening, Katie?" he asked.

"They're going to Canada, Siggi. They'll become Canadians and they'll work hard and help build Canada into a wonderful country."

"Why's that boy so sad?" asked Siggi. He pointed at Nicholas, who was boarding with others from the orphanage, his head down, not looking at his mother whose shoulders shook with weeping.

"He doesn't want to leave his mother. He's someone very important in your life, Siggi. Don't worry. His story has a happy ending. He'll marry a wonderful person. And he'll become your great-great-grandfather." When she saw Siggi's blank look, she said, "When we're home I'll explain it all to you."

As Katie and Siggi watched the line of children slowly boarding, Mother James came running up to Miss Charity, grabbed her by the shoulder, and started shouting. Her children stopped at the sound of her voice. Their rosy cheeks blanched. But they must have realized that Mother James wasn't likely to hit them in front of Miss Charity, for, quite soon, their expressions changed to actual pleasure at seeing her. Katie wasn't really surprised. She knew when she had been frightened, as Mother James's children must feel now, she had wanted nothing more than to be with her parents. As the children faced the prospect of being wrenched from everything they knew, they'd want their mother, no matter what that mother was like.

Katie couldn't hear much of what Mother James said to Miss

Charity, but she saw the giant woman's demeanour change. Katie heard her loud voice clearly, "Well, if yur sure they'll 'ave better lives," before she slouched away and Miss Charity hurried the children onto the ship.

As she watched Mother James walk sadly away from her children, Katie reconsidered her opinion of her. She knew gin was a terrible addiction. She had seen the woman's sudden changes in mood and figured this was because of the drink. Mother James clearly wanted a better life for her children than she could give them. Katie knew firsthand from her weeks as Stevie how difficult it was to fight the struggles of a life in poverty.

Peggy shook her bridle and soared into the silent sky, beginning the journey back to their own time, taking Katie and Siggi back to their own family.

When Peggy started circling again, Katie knew they were home. The pony landed in Haggarty's field. The Yukon was crisp with cold, for no time had passed while they were gone. The air smelled so clean—no coal smoke pollution here! It was still winter. The snowbanks were white with fresh snow.

After seeing Peggy contented in her stall, the children excitedly ran back to the cabin to be with their parents. Marc and Maggie opened their arms to them both. Siggi was so excited, he shouted, "Mom, Dad, Katie saved me! Her pony can fly! Where's Skippy?" The child wiggled out of his parents' arms and ran off to find his dog. Katie felt a calm happiness at being in this snug, cheerful cabin once again.

A couple of days later, after much telling of the details of what had happened, Katie saw that her parents were sneaking peeks at her to see how she felt about Siggi now, perhaps afraid that she'd fall back into her old anger and resentment. So she decided to do something to convince them that she really did accept him as part of the family. She could explain until the cows came home, but she had to show her parents that she'd changed.

The four of them were sitting at the table, still talking, talking, talking, when she ran to her room and came back with the Victorian book, the dolls, and the box full of clothes.

"Katie, what are you doing?" asked Maggie in an anxious voice.

"Here, take this," Katie said, handing the book, the dolls, and the box to her mother. "You've kept them all these years—they really belong to you. Thanks for giving them to me. I liked them a lot, but I don't need another family now," she said. "I've got mine right here." She turned to Siggi, and to his surprise, hugged him.

"That's a gift to us, Katie," said Mom, sudden tears springing to her eyes. After what seemed like a long time, she went on. "Thanks for the book. It's always meant a lot to me, but it means even more now. We have a gift for you, too." She gave Katie a wrapped present.

Katie ripped off the paper to reveal a small box. Inside was a silver locket, a replica of the one she had lost. She opened it with her thumbnail and there, inside a heart-shaped inner compartment, was a picture of her parents and their two children, Katie and Siggi, standing in front of a shaggy Icelandic pony.

"I'll wear it always," she said solemnly, as Mom helped her fasten it around her neck.

Siggi jumped up in the happy, exuberant way he'd had in England, almost upsetting his chair so it rocked from front legs to back before settling with a thump.

"I wanna take Skippy out to play now," he said. "Wanna come, Katie?"

"Not now," she answered. "I think I'll go and see how Peggy's doing."

"Peggy, Peggy, Peggy," Siggi said. "You've got horses on the brain."

Mom looked disappointed. "Katie, can't you play with Siggi for twenty minutes or so before you go to Haggarty's? He's just a little boy, after all."

Katie paused a minute. "I'll stay here and play with Siggi and Skippy for a while," she agreed, "if Siggi will help me with my chores in the barn."

"I think that's a good plan," said Dad.

Katie gave Siggi a little shove and said, "I mean help—not just stand around watching me. You're big enough now to do some real work."

She turned to her parents. "If you want a family discussion on adoption, I'm all for it," she said.

Siggi wasn't listening. He was making a face at Katie, thinking Mom and Dad wouldn't see. Katie saw, but she didn't feel one bit angry. After all, Siggi was just a little boy.

"I guess we're a real family now, huh?" she asked Mom and Dad.

Mom started to giggle. Then, as Dad chuckled, too, she laughed out loud. When they heard this, Katie and Siggi couldn't help but join in. Soon all four of them were laughing helplessly—together.